dark

dark

kenji jasper

broadway books
new york

an [s]affiliated book

dark

a novel

kenji jasper

broadway books
new york
an [s]affiliated book

An [S]Affiliated Book.

Broadway Books titles may be purchased for business or
promotional use or for special sales. For information, please write
to: Special Markets Department, Random House, Inc., 1540
Broadway, New York, NY 10036.

BROADWAY BOOKS and its logo, a letter B bisected on the diagonal, are
trademarks of Broadway Books, a division of Random House, Inc.

Visit our website at www.broadwaybooks.com

This book is a work of fiction. Names, characters, businesses,
organizations, places, events, and incidents either are the product of
the author's imagination or are used fictitiously. Any resemblance to
actual persons, living or dead, events, or locales is entirely coincidental.

Library of Congress Cataloging-in-Publication Data
Jasper, Kenji.
Dark: a novel / Kenji Jasper.—1st ed.
p. cm.
1. Shaw (Washington, D.C.)—Fiction. 2. Afro-American men—
Fiction. 3. Male friendship—Fiction. 4. Violence—Fiction. I. Title.
PS3560.A67 D37 2001
813'.6—dc21   00-046808

FIRST EDITION

Designed by Jennifer Ann Daddio

ISBN 0-7679-0707-8

1 3 5 7 9 10 8 6 4 2

for greg, khari, rob, brian, sparky,

and the crew we all used to be

acknowledgments

(Only a few are in any specific order)

i have to thank the creator,
God my Father, for the many blessings He bestows upon me daily, Mom, Pop, Carla, Annia, Imani, Li'l Jay, Tony and Grandma Sally, my editor Gerald Howard for believing in my work enough to put up with all it took for me to get on at Broadway Books, my attorney Georgia Murray for getting the *or*deal done, Deb, all of my editorial readers: Tiffany Thompson, Becca Konata, Ms. Inge, and Tasha Harris. Much thanks to my trainer Nic Stevens, Lisa Pegram, Dr. Cindy Lutenbacher, Cipher (Mill, Shell, Juba, Gaff, Okorie,

and Anika) for sharing their creative tables with me, Natalie and Gabrielle LaRochelle, Coco and Joshua White, Damon Gunn, Chris Yates, Mike Karoma, my sisters Cheryl Smith and Rebeccah Bennett, Maybelle Bennett, Mr. Keith Wasserman, Mr. Stephen Pratt, Mr. Ken Cooper, Ms. Sheila Solomon, Mrs. Mary Curtis, Mr. Bob Meadows, Professor Judy Gebre-Hewitt, Professor Kimberly Wallace Sanders, Audrey Irons, Tahra, Knox, Ro and Dave, Demetrius Pace, Bob Morales, Sabina and Erin, D-Gunn, Kerry Walker, Larmarrous and Katrisa Shirley (sorry if I mispelled y'all's names), the Caped Crusaders (Mike, Murph, and Mark), everybody that knew me from growing up in Fairfax Village and Hillcrest: Mark, Bo, Damon Williams, Damon Hudson, Butchie, Nyere, John, and Rocky (R.I.P.). Much love to everyone who loves me. And of course I can't forget Marc Gerald, for seeing a good thing and running with it. Until . . .

dark

prologue

Pop:

It's Monday morning. I'm about to leave and I'm down here trying to figure out how this is going to end. And when you're at the point that I've reached you see that being a man isn't easy. Now I see what you meant when you used to talk about hindsight being 20/20. If I had known that I was going to walk in on Sierra and Nick I wouldn't have even gone over to her house that day. If I had known that I was going to pull that trigger I never would've gone to that party. And if I had known that taking a week's vacation was going to change my life forever I definitely would've gone sooner.

See, Pop, I've spent my whole life living on our block thinking that there wasn't anywhere else to go. I didn't think that there were other cities, or different kinds of people or fine older women who came to your door in the middle of the night looking to get some. I didn't know that there were crazy fools running around who would do anything for love, maybe even kill, and I especially didn't know the truth about my mama, the truth you had kept from me for my whole life.

I've learned so much in this past week. I've learned what it feels like to be possessed by revenge and to make love on a living room carpet. I've learned that there are people who go to sleep with ghosts over their beds at night and they drink them away whenever they get the chance. There are people who kill for nothing and live for nothing but themselves. They say it's a small world but after this past week I'm not ready to believe it.

But see, now that I know all these things I don't know what to do with them. I got a bunch of choices to make that nobody can help me with. Even Snowflake, E, and Ray Ray can't get me out of having to find my way in life. Neither can you.

I don't know if I'm going to mail this. But I just want you to know that I've learned everything you taught me.

Love,
Thai

start

of the four of us,
I was the smart one. I did the best in school, I got a few
awards, and I even got to introduce Mayor Barry when he
came to visit my junior high school. E was the lucky one.
Everything always went his way no matter what the odds
were. Ray Ray was the crazy one. He would do anything just
for the rush. He'd smash somebody in the mouth at a party a
half a city away from home just to see the look on the man's
face when he took that first hit. But Snowflake was the bad
one. He did what he wanted. And when you were around

him, you did what he wanted too. If you didn't he caused problems. Even though he was our main boy, we didn't want any problems from him.

We all lived in Shaw. And Shaw was a place where you didn't come to play around. The threat of bullets and beatdowns always hung in the air like the smell of burning tar. If you walked by the right building at the right time you might hear the Williamses arguing about their son Damien's crack habit or Mr. Harris on the third floor yelling at the newspaper about how the Redskins wouldn't make it to another Super Bowl in his lifetime. Or there was always Frank, who spent his days over on the playground impressing the little kids by showing them the bullet scar on his calf and the chrome-plated 9mm that gave him the scar when he dropped it on the ground while running from someone he owed money to.

But Shaw was a little different than a lot of the other neighborhoods in Northwest. We went hard but we weren't anything like the cats down in Southeast or the ones in Northeast off of Montana Avenue. We were right between downtown and U Street, trapped between the suit-and-tie DC you saw in the movies and the place people burned down after they killed Martin Luther King long before I was born. To me that made us special, something more than just another name they called out at the go-go clubs on Saturday nights.

If anybody asked us, that was where we said we were from. Shaw was what we represented, just like the dudes over in the Capper projects or anybody who lived in Le Droit

Park. For us life started and stopped in those three or four blocks that surrounded the neighborhood playground, even though downtown DC was just a few blocks away. If anybody had something to say about our neighborhood it came to warnings, blows, or bullets. That worked both ways. But what happened wasn't about us or the neighborhood. It was about me.

Freddy was dead. A kid named Aaron had shot two bullets into his face outside of the Marlow Heights movie theater two days before on the hottest Tuesday of the summer. It was Thursday and the funeral was the next morning. But that night Freddy's little brother Daron and all his cousins threw a "rest in peace" party in their basement in Congress Heights on the other side of the city. They threw a party while their mama was upstairs crying her eyes out and mumbling to herself about what to do now that her first boy was gone. She had even told a neighbor she was thinking about walking down to the precinct with Freddy's old .38 to shoot Aaron while he was still in the holding cell. I heard all of that in the car on the way to the party.

I didn't know Freddy or Aaron or Daron or his mama or the name of the girl who opened up the front door for us. But Freddy was Snowflake's cousin and Snowflake was my boy and we were both from Shaw, so I rolled wherever he needed me to be.

I, Thai Williams, the smart one, however, had plenty on my mind. Three hours before I'd chased a light-skinned pretty boy named Nick through and out of Wheaton Plaza before he turned around and opened fire on Snowflake and me with a .22. Two days before he had fucked my girl in her living room fifteen minutes before the time I was supposed to show up. I came early. He didn't cum at all.

We found out that he worked at the Gap in Wheaton and decided to pay him a visit with three more of Shaw's finest to express our disappointment with him. Snowflake had wanted me to kill him from the start. But I wasn't a killer. I convinced him to settle for an ass-whipping in a public place.

I just wanted him to know that I wasn't the one to mess with. He had fucked my girl on the same floor in the same room where my baby was conceived, before it died. I put all of that on Nick's head when I walked into the Gap with three other people behind me.

When he saw me he broke for the back door. Snowflake and I chased him out the back and through the parking lot until he pulled that .22 and let off five shots in our direction. He shattered a few car windows but missed us completely and then disappeared. That's what had happened several hours before I walked into Freddy's "rest in peace" party.

But despite everything I've just told you I don't want you to get the wrong idea about me. I wasn't the kind of dude you saw getting stuffed into police cars on the evening news, and neither was E. Sure Ray Ray and Snowflake were knuckleheads, but when the time came to do their dirt they always kept us out of it. E and I did our homework and got our diplomas and talked about going to college. Ray Ray and Snowflake listened and told us to do what we had to do to get it done. But the summer after graduation something unexpected happened. E left.

dark

His mama, who was Indian, popped up after fourteen years and asked him to move to Charlotte with her and help her with her real estate business. The crazier thing was that E said yes. He left and I had to fend for myself. So after working my eight-hour days at the Department of Public Works I spent my nights with the crazy one and the bad one and that night they had brought me to the party to forget about Wheaton Plaza.

I could see the force the girl was using to grind her plump derrière against me as I danced behind her. But I didn't feel it. I was miles away from the dark cramped basement where my dark body was moving to the beat of the Backyard Band tape that played through the blown speakers. I thought about what had happened earlier in the day and earlier in the week. What had I done to make Sierra want to disrespect me like that? I had called every other day and I took her out when I could and when she was pregnant I made her my life, only to have her put a knife through my heart, twist it, and set it on fire. Now a coldness ran through me, as if my veins were filled with ice water. So while I danced with that girl with the big booty, pretending like nothing was wrong, I knew that something was about to happen.

In the dim basement light I could see Snowflake and Ray Ray and Ray's cousin Cuckoo on the other side of the room drinking the punch that was more Absolut than anything else. The song changed and I walked over to them and planted my roots in their line of wallflowers.

"You all right?" Cuckoo asked me.

We called him Cuckoo because he was crazy, crazier than Ray Ray. From what I had heard he was a killer. He pulled triggers for whoever could afford it, even for some of the Koreans way out in Maryland. He was Ray's cousin, and his inspiration for being crazy. Whenever he came through the neighborhood it either meant a lot of laughs or a lot of drama.

"Yeah, I'm straight," I said back to him.

"Don't worry. We gonna get dat nigga. He from around this way too. He ain't got no time."

I didn't say anything. I didn't really want Nick to die and I really didn't want to kill him. But I was stuck on Sierra, and I wondered why she had made me do all of this. I wanted revenge to replace something else. But all of that aside, Cuckoo was right. Nick was living on borrowed time. I hoped that he'd called into the Gap to say he'd quit because a day wouldn't go by when somebody could have been waiting for him.

Nick had had on an Anacostia b-ball jersey when he did a Michael Johnson out of Sierra's house. So I knew what school he went to. Unless he was getting a new name and a new face, the fact of the matter was that he had shot at Snowflake and Snow always said that if somebody shot at him he'd shoot right back.

"Damn, this nigga Freddy knew everybody. All these people came for him and he dead," I said to Cuckoo. I was about to light a cigarette but I'd left my lighter in the car. dark

"He was the man up at Anacostia. He used to start on the hoops squad at erry game," he replied.

The word "Anacostia" echoed in my head. I saw Nick's jersey on Sierra's floor right next to their naked bodies. Then like the Flash he threw it on, pulled his shorts, and ran out. And as if on cue, right after that very image, was when it started.

"Wassup nigga!" a voice yelled over the music on the other side of the room. I couldn't see who the voice belonged to in the dark but I heard him slapping five with someone else. He was too loud. I turned to Cuckoo.

"You know dat nigga?" I asked.

"Nah," he said, "but he rollin' up in here like he's the man or somethin' when Freddy's supposed to be the man tonight."

"You right," I said. Cuckoo turned to Snowflake and mumbled something. Snowflake nodded to him and took a puff from the blunt Ray Ray had rolled in the car. Then the go-go tape cut off and the basement lights came up. "Hey, somebody tell that nigga Nick he left his lights on!" Daron yelled.

First people giggled and then there were a few shouts to turn the music back on. But for the four of us time stood still. The basement lights went back out. But before they did we had seen him and he couldn't have been more than five feet in front us.

He was talking to the girl who I had just finished dancing with and he had on the same shirt and slacks from the mall. The rest of the wallflowers turned to me with a knowing look. But I didn't know what they were looking for me to do. I was busy dwelling on the fact that he had been stupid enough to show up at a party after he'd let off shots at four dudes he didn't know in the middle of one of the biggest malls in the DC metropolitan area. Our city was too small for that.

We could have been anybody. That was the underlying rule in DC. The enemy was everywhere except for on your own block, but you even had to watch your back there. The enemy could turn up sitting behind you in the movies or he could be bagging your groceries or sitting across from you at your main boy's dinner table. But he was always at the parties, especially that one party where you least expected him to show up.

In the low light I watched Nick's profile shift and turn. Watching his bald peanut head made me cut back to the same footage of him on top of Sierra on the living room floor with Jodeci playing in the background. I didn't remember the song but I knew it was Jodeci. He did that Michael Johnson through the back and off of the porch and I didn't chase after him. That was where my movie memory had stopped. I ran that same snippet over and over again as I watched him shift and bob his head to the music.

I watched until I couldn't watch anymore. I wanted to move and something moved me. Something took my body and pushed it past two or three people and that something led my right fist to crack across his jaw and make it rattle. But he was ready and he tagged me back and we traded blows until I was on top of him, punching into the blackness of the carpet, connecting only once or twice.

A foot kicked me in the back and I knew that Nick hadn't

come alone. But that was the only foot I felt, which meant that my boys were doing their job. Nick pushed me off of him and scrambled away. As I began my pursuit through the parting crowd someone on my team placed something heavy in my left fist. I carried that something heavy with me when the crawl turned into a chase out the back and through the yard.

I tripped over a wood bench and fell into the sparse grass while he went over the fence. I got to my feet and kicked the back gate open and barely missed his left hook. He had been waiting for me on the other side. I tagged him with a hard jab of my own and he hit the pavement flat on his back. I looked and there was a gleaming chrome .380 in my grip.

He had seen the gun before I had. I saw the recognition on his face that I could take his life. He lay there like a deer staring into headlights wondering if this was it or if he'd live to be a light-skinned pretty boy for one more day.

I wanted to say something but I didn't have the words. I didn't feel anything except for the fresh blood running down my lip. He'd gotten me good. He'd really gotten me good. He'd fucked my girl (who after the fact had more or less told me she never wanted to see me again). He'd outrun me on two occasions. He'd shot at me and most recently punched me in the mouth in the middle of a house party. But I wasn't stuck on those things. I was stuck on him being inside of Sierra, him being in the place where my baby was born, and while I was stuck on that I pulled the trigger and blew a hole in his head, a lake of crimson forming on the pavement beneath his lifeless skull.

It took me more than a few seconds to realize this wasn't something I was watching on TV. I had seen it before in real life but I was never a participant. Even though the gun was hot I still felt the ice water rushing through my veins and arteries.

Murder wasn't what I had meant to do when I kicked that fence open. It definitely wasn't what I had to do. But I had done it and I had to deal. Multiple hands pulled me into the back of Snowflake's station wagon. They took the gun away and I stared at Nick's corpse as it grew further and further away from me down the alley. I tried to close my eyes but I was too scared to stop looking. Those multiple hands pulled me into the back of the wagon, and after nineteen years and three months they'd finally brought me into the dark.

dark

dining

"i hope you're not afraid
of the dark," she said to me as I stood in the doorway of her apartment and watched her light the candles. I don't remember what I said in reply, but whatever it was made her laugh. I wasn't pressed to make her laugh. I was even less pressed about being there: in the doorway of a white girl's apartment in a town I didn't know.

She wasn't the black white but the whiter-than-white white. She was the white that was so white that I found myself thinking about the *Partridge Family* or *90210* and *Party of*

Five on Wednesday nights. Plus she had this fake-naive look plastered across her white face that let me know that if I was down to switch teams, she'd at least be willing to polish my bat. I was fine with the team I was on. And while I could talk all day about the intensity of her whiteness the reality was that she was human, breathing, and she had a pulse. She had offered me a home-cooked meal after I'd driven seven hours on I-85 with nothing to eat except for what I could find in gas stations. I had wanted to get to Charlotte before the dark hit.

She glided to each corner of the studio like a ghost. Her lighter bounced off of the clusters of scented candles and set the room ablaze. I stayed put in the doorway and contemplated whether or not I should just walk down the one flight of stairs to the emptiness of my new place or whether I should stay and get my grub on. I didn't want the neighbors to think I had jungle fever. But I wanted to eat. She had food. I stayed where I was.

It was strange to just stand when I'd spent the last two days in perpetual motion. I'd been packing bags, screening calls, and making excuses so that I could make the trip. The worry was that the trip might make me into a fugitive.

"So what are you doing in Charlotte?" she asked me as I closed the door and made my way towards the fluorescent-yellow beanbag chair next to the window. It was a nice window, a big wide bay one overlooking Tryon Street. I sat and lost myself in the eerie way the candlelight illuminated the art d a r k on the opposite wall, reflecting on how I had ended up at her place.

"Just down here to see my friend," I replied. "He moved down here a year ago and I decided to spend my vacation hangin' out wit' him. His mom owns the buildin'."

"Oh, that Indian lady. I never remember her name."

"Neither do I," I said in hopes of moving away from the topic.

The white girl had seen me emptying out the trunk of my Maxima when she was coming in from the neighbor-hood gym and had decided to be friendly. Her idea of being friendly was to spend most of our conversation telling me about how she was trying to quit her bartending job at a strip club for something less immoral. I gave her the nods and the yesses she needed to feel like I really cared and the next thing I knew I was following her up the steps to her apartment on the third floor. Still dressed in her amply filled sports bra and tights, she clattered a few pots on the stove and asked me if I liked chicken parmigiana. I nodded even though I'd never had it before. Like most white girls she didn't have much of a booty. So there was that much less to entertain me while she cooked. I closed my eyes and without wanting to went back into the nightmare.

Three days, a .380, and one shot had brought me to Charlotte at the end of the summer when I should've been trying to start college at UDC in the spring. I had put college off since graduation. If I didn't start soon it was only a matter of time before I let it go completely.

"So do you have a girlfriend?" she asked as we took seats at the neatly set table.

"Nah, but I ain't lookin' for one either," I replied.

16

"Why's that?" she asked.

" 'Cuz they don't seem to bring me nothing but trouble."

"Or do you just let them get you in trouble?" She gave me a joker-faced grin but my eyes buried themselves back in my empty plate.

After the deed was done on the night in question, Snowflake's wagon had taken twenty twists and turns through the unfamiliar streets of Southeast. Then Snow pulled us into Anacostia Park, took the .380 from Cuckoo, got out, and tossed it into the river like a pebble. Then he got back in the car and we headed towards the freeway that led us home.

I was scared, but I wasn't trembling the way I had been at first. I didn't know what to tell Pop or how many people in that party might snitch or how I was going to get out of town without losing the best job I'd had in my nineteen years. Every voice in the car had an opinion, but I turned deaf to every single one because none of their opinions made any sense. But by the time I put my key in the front door I knew I would tell Pop that I was going down to visit E for a few days because I had to use my vacation time and the summer was almost over. I would call the job and say I needed to take my vacation without notice for a family emergency. Since I'd done more in my department in a year than some had done in three, my supervisor would cut me some slack. Then I would call E and tell him that I needed a place to lay low. He always came through, and this would be no exception. I dark couldn't tell him the meat of the matter over the phone. The cops could have already had it tapped. Some loudmouthed cat from the party might have already been giving the cops a description. They could have been already dragging the river for the gun.

"I just broke up with my boyfriend," she said as she poured herself another glass of wine, "and I'm not looking for another one either. It seems like love makes everything way more complicated."

"I couldn't tell you nothin' 'bout that. I ain't never been in love."

Shock washed over the fake-naive look on her face and her jaw drooped.

"You've never been in love?" she asked, sounding like a dumb blonde with hair dyed a deep brunette.

"Nope, and I don't think I'm missin' anything. From what I know, love make you do stupid shit and I've done enough stupid shit already."

E called me back the next morning and told me he'd sent a FedEx with a set of keys and the address to one of the apartment buildings his mother owned. It was on the porch the next morning. E always knew how to hook it up.

But getting that envelope was the only time I stepped out of the house for those two days. I spent most of the time up in my room. I tried to sleep for as long as I could but kept seeing the blood oozing onto the sidewalk and that final look on Nick's face, a last appeal for mercy that went unheeded. I smoked the last of a dime bag Snow had given me a week before, but it never got me off the ground. I imagined SWAT teams gathering just outside the front gate. I pictured Nick's brother or cousin or maybe even his high school counselor loading up the artillery and coming after all of us. I imagined a drive-by where we all got killed. They would even find Cuckoo out in Maryland. I knew fate had both feet on the gas and would pop the curb to drive straight into my living room. I didn't even think I'd live long enough to see that envelope on the porch. But when it came I knew it was time for me to go.

"So is this your first apartment?" she asked me.

"Yeah, first time I ever left home. But it's just me and my pops at home, and he works all the time. So I been on my own before."

"So you don't get lonely?"

"I don't know," I said, thinking about it. "For me that was always the way it was. It was always just me and maybe my boys. So I guess I ain't ever had enough people around me to make me know what lonely feels like."

"You regret that?"

"That's just the way it was. I don't really regret nothin'. Well, almost nothin'."

Then dinner was served and as I sat at the white girl's dinner table two hours after I had gotten into town, I still didn't have it all together and I felt like it showed. My clothes stuck to me from the humidity and I had been chain-smoking Newports for more than thirty-six hours. I just needed to lay low. But I hadn't expected that anyone else would be there, that others would be trying to lay low with me.

The white white girl was named Qualie Madison. She dark hated her name. She'd learned to cook chicken parmigiana from her mother when she was fifteen and she wanted to be an accountant when she finished school. She was twenty and she had moved in a month before me to the day and she said that she liked it, even though her parents said that all the black people in the building made them uncomfortable.

"So what are you going to be doing down here?" she asked cheerfully while pouring me another glass of wine. I had never actually had wine before, not good wine at least. I took gulps instead of civilized sips. My idea of drinking was getting faded off of malt liquor at a party or in front of some-body's building and then throwing up on the sidewalk across the street from my house at the end of the night. Now in Charlotte I was having wine with dinner. Up until then I thought that was the kind of thing that only happened in those three-floor townhouses up on 16th Street where all the paid people lived. I definitely was not at home.

"Just chillin' with my man. But . . . so . . . are you from here?" I asked to show her that I was actually interested in the conversation. I spoke with my eyes still focused on my nearly cleaned plate. She giggled and shook her head. Her buzz was obvious.

"No, I'm from Chattanooga, but my folks and me moved up here when I was in high school."

"What's the difference between here and Chattanooga?" I asked.

From what I knew, everything in the South was the same. It was all supposed to be dirt roads and tobacco fields.

"Charlotte's going somewhere. Chattanooga isn't," she replied matter-of-factly.

There was this tension around her eyes that told me she

was somewhere west of the truth. She was telling me what she thought I wanted to hear. That bothered me even though I was doing the same thing.

Charlotte was the furthest I had ever been outside of DC. The city seemed artificial, like it had been grown in a lab. It didn't have a voice or a tradition. But at least it was quiet.

From the highway all I could see was suburban turf. There were stretches of houses and trees and shopping areas and grocery stores. But then it looked like they had just dropped six or seven blocks of large buildings and tall sky-scrapers in the middle of it so that they could call it a city. That didn't fit. When I drove through what they called downtown a little after seven, it had been deserted. There wasn't a single person on the street. To me that wasn't how real cities were. It definitely wasn't like that at home.

E's mama's apartment building was on Tryon Street. Tryon stretched from the middle of downtown all the way out into the suburbs by UNC Charlotte. It was one of a few remaining buildings that sat on the thin line of structures be-tween the mostly suburban and supposedly urban parts of Charlotte. I had never seen buildings as tall as downtown Charlotte's before. But that still didn't make Charlotte a real city.

But to be honest, I wasn't concerned about Charlotte and it's pseudo-city status. I didn't think I could find anywhere on the planet that was better than home. I had everything I needed on *my* block and in *my* city.

Qualie said that when she graduated from high school it was like she finally had a chance to see the world. For us graduation just meant that you stopped going to school and you started working. That was it and that was why it surprised all of us when E decided to break the mold.

Her hair was cut a little shorter than a bob, like a black girl's, and her eyes were a creamy green like jade. I was sure plenty of men had wanted her. She looked like a girl I might have seen on the movie of the week playing somebody's too-stupid-for-her-own-good mistress. I hadn't been that close to that kind of girl before, and the words flying out of her mouth meant almost nothing to me most of the time we talked. But I wanted to know more about her world, the one I never wanted to live in.

"I know you're barely moved in and all. You can stay up here tonight if you like. I have a sofa bed. . . ."

"Nah, that's all right," I said. "My apartment's got furniture in it, so all I gotta do is lay down."

"You sure?" she asked. "I don't have to go to work tomorrow."

"Nah, I'm all right," I said. "So what school you say you went to?"

"UNC Charlotte. It's really nice. I wish I could go full-time, but I gotta pay the bills, you know. Maybe if I get a scholarship or somethin' I will, but I'm just getting started, so I want to take my time."

"Don't work too hard," I said. I had cleaned my plate, and every few minutes I peeked over at the stove to see if there was any more left. From what I could see the pan looked empty. I frowned.

"I just keep working at it, because I don't want to be bartending in strip clubs for the rest of my life."

"My pop's a bartender. There's worse jobs you can have."

"I didn't mean it like that. I'm not even a good bartender. I mess up drinks all the time."

I had had five glasses of wine and my head felt like a cinder block. I started looking at the door, but I didn't want to move. The drive and the stress and all the cigarettes had taken their toll. Her couch started to sound like a good move.

"My pop never messed up a drink," I said. "He likes drinking too much."

"Is he an alcoholic?" she asked.

"Nah, nothin' like that. But he can drink a lot, though. He likes mixing things together to see what he can come up with. He always tries to come up with somethin' special."

"Can you make anything special?" she asked. It wasn't what she said but the way she said it. She had leaned her body towards me as the words parted her lips, as if my answer would take our dinner to some new level. That was when I knew it was time for me to leave.

"Thanks for the dinner, but I'm 'bout to be out," I said as I struggled to get up. My legs felt like they might fold under me, but they held.

"You sure you don't want to . . ."

"Nah, I'm 'bout to get some sleep," I said. She practically had to jog to catch me as I got to the door.

"Well, maybe we can get together again sometime."

"I don't think so," I said, "but I'll probably see you

dark

around." I closed the door behind me and in her face at the same time.

My head felt twenty pounds lighter in the hallway. I had killed a man and I didn't know what to think about it. She had cooked me dinner hoping to get something else, and I don't think she knew what to think about it. I'd never had dinner with anyone white before. To me all white people were like her, ghosts that lit candles in their apartments and felt uncomfortable in my neighborhood. I wasn't looking forward to dining with them again.

The apartment was the same as it was two hours before. In the dark I found my way over to my duffel bag and took out the Beretta. It was heavy in my hand. I tucked it behind the pillow on the futon. I didn't feel safe, but I was too tired to care.

Ray Ray had given the gun to me in my room right before I was about to leave. It was his favorite gun, and 9mms weren't cheap to come across. It was brand-new and had never been fired, and he wanted me to have it.

"If you get into some shit I want you to do it how we do it," he said as I tucked the piece into my bag.

"Hopefully there won't be nothin' to get into," I said. "I been in enough already."

I slapped his hand and locked it with mine, and in ten minutes I was on my way towards 95 South.

But holding it was all it took. Whenever I even touched the steel I was back in that Congress Heights alley trying to recall how it had happened so fast. Part of me had a permanent residence there. After all, it had been Nick's fault.

Hadn't it? He had pushed me further than I'd ever gone. He'd fucked my girl and he'd shot at Snowflake and he was the kind of pretty mothafucka that got on my nerves just for existing. That was the how when and why and enough to switch all my morals off. But now my morals were back in place and I was on the run. The run was going to kill me slowly.

When I stretched out on the futon my eyelids were propped open by an unknown force. I was up for another hour before the darkness in front of my eyes started to blur. I heard the voices in the darkness of that basement and I felt my finger tighten on that trigger followed by the kick from the pistol as it fired once. "It only takes one shot," Pop used to tell me. He was right.

monday

the noise at the door

sharpened the darkened room into focus. When the dead bolt clicked I tumbled into paranoia and grabbed for the Beretta under the pillow. I had it cocked and aimed by the time the door creaked open.

"You better get the fuck outta here!" I said loudly. My heart beat like a kick-drum.

"Good thing I wasn't the super," the voice replied calmly.

It was a voice I knew as well as my own. It had a little

26

more bass and a tiny bit of a southern twang, but I knew it was E. I let out a sigh of relief and lowered the pistol.

"Nigga, don't you know how to knock?" I asked.

"Not when I got a key to every apartment in the building. Shit, you should be lettin' *me* shoot *your* ass after what I went through to get you in here. Moms must really love me to let me give up one of her places when she only met you once."

In the dark there seemed to be miles and years between us, even though it was really only a few feet and a few months since he'd come back to the neighborhood for New Year's. The silhouette of his arm dug into his left pants pocket. There was a flicking sound and a stream of flame rose from his fist that momentarily gave his bearded face an orange glow while he lit his cigarette. He had on a shirt and tie and dress pants. Looking at him I almost forgot that he and I had run the neighborhood together for most of our lives.

In the dark he walked back towards the doorway, where the light from the hall crept into the room. I got up and followed. The light hurt my eyes but they adjusted.

Enrique hated the dark. He used to leave all three lights on in his room at night while he slept. I think it was psychological. Before he moved to Shaw, he told me, he had spent close to a month living in a one-room studio apartment with no lights over in Southeast because of some problem his dad had with the power company or the landlord or somebody. After something like that I'd always keep the lights on too.

"I gotta thank your moms for lookin' out," I said as I tucked the gun into my shorts. I felt along the wall for the light switch and found it. The ceiling light washed over the room, and E sighed for relief and moved back into the apartment.

His cornrows were gone with only a close Caesar in their place. He had gotten a little taller and he wasn't as skinny as I remembered him. Instead of the old E he came off like a fifth-grader who'd been stuck in his picture-day clothes for an extra nine years.

"So what's up? What's all this surprise-visit stuff about?" He sat down and folded his jacket over the arm of the couch.

"It's a long story," I said. My stomach growled even though the chicken parmigiana hadn't fully digested. "Get me sumpin' to eat and I'll break it down for you."

"You tryin' to eat in Charlotte at eleven o'clock at night in the middle of the week? We ain't got too many choices except for IHOP or somethin'."

"You know I don't care," I replied, resigned to consume anything edible.

"Then let's roll," he said grinning as we jetted out. I locked the door behind me.

The first time I met E he almost whipped my ass in a fight on the playground. He had just moved on the block from Southeast and I'd decided to show him that being down with the neighborhood was a privilege you had to earn. He called next on the basketball court while we were playing and when his time came I knocked his skinny nine-year-old frame down on the first play. After twenty seconds of talking out of the sides of our necks I hit him. Then he hit me. Then I hit him again. But he just kept coming back, each time faster and stronger.

Kenny and Frank and some of the other little dudes I hung with tried to jump in, but I signaled them to back off. After I blocked his last blow and connected with mine I told him that he was cool. He obviously didn't get that it was over, because he kept staring at all of us like we were about to kill him. He had fought for his life while I had taken it as just another scrap. That was the difference between us.

He started coming over to my house. I went to see him and his dad over at their apartment, and by the time the sixth grade rolled around if you saw one of us and not the other there was a problem. We were two parts of the same whole, little ghetto boys looking for mothers that weren't around, and neither of us wanted to end up like the kids that got sent to Oakhill and receiving homes and never came back.

E's sparkling periwinkle 4Runner was double-parked in front of the building. The humidity outside made the air so thick that it could have been liquid. I might not have been so hot if I wasn't wearing a black T-shirt, jeans, and boots in the stifling heat.

His jeep was perfect. It was buffed and polished like a trophy, and I was a little jealous when I compared it to my '88 Maxima with the missing hubcap that was parked a few cars down. Before I saw him I'd been happy to have new tires, but E had a brand-new ride.

He turned on the radio and the Wu-Tang Clan shredded the silence. I fiddled with the Newport he had given me on the stairwell and pushed in the lighter next to the ashtray. dark Then we pulled off.

"What you so nervous about?" he asked me, his eyes focused on the road the whole time. "You only play wit' your smokes when you nervous."

"I'll tell you about it when we get there," I said as I pulled the lighter out and lit the cigarette. A thin puff of smoke pushed its way between my lips and hung in the hot liquid air.

"You don't even know where we're goin'," he replied.

"Wit' everything I been through it don't make no difference. Long as it's gonna be food." I looked out the window at the barren streets. We drove past the moonlit silhouettes of a few abandoned buildings and warehouses. Everything seemed dead. I once again asked myself what I was doing there and what I could possibly find five hundred miles from home.

"It sure as hell ain't home, is it?" Enrique said as if he'd read my mind. I figured with me sitting there he was imagining his new city through my eyes.

"At home this time of night in the summer, shit is just gettin' started. You know, last summer when I first got here and me and Ma used to get into fights all the time, I'd go out, but I could never find anything to do. So I'd just end up drivin' forever. It ain't been easy getting used to livin' here. After all, when I first came down I sorta hated my moms. Well, anyway, Charlotte ain't DC."

"Ain't dat the truth."

There was very little in my life I hadn't done without him there. I remembered the many nights he and I had spent stretched out on my porch trying to get sober before we faced our fathers. He had more to worry about. His dad had been an

30

alcoholic. My dad was a bartender. What could Pop really say to me? But still, I didn't want to press my luck. And that had all happened in a different place, a different life for him.

"You like it down here?" I asked him as we turned onto Interstate 77.

"It's good and it's bad," he said, grinning to himself. "It's safe down here. Not like they *don't* be shooting as much here. Plus nobody knows me. I ain't got nothin' to worry about like I do at home, and when I'm out workin', even the white boys call me Mr. Mitchell."

"That sound all right to me. Don't nobody call me nothin' at my job."

"Man, names don't mean nothin'. We both gettin' pay-checks at the end of the week, and that's all that matters. But I ain't gon' lie. I kinda miss home. I miss it every day." He reached for my cigarette and took a drag. "So what you here for, anyway?"

I paused for a minute, unsure of whether or not he wanted the long or the short version. I wasn't even sure of which was which myself.

"Just tryin' to chill out for a second," I replied as I exhaled another whirling cloud of smoke. This time it got sucked out of the open window. "Guess you don't like to use the air?"

"Burns up your gas, and jeeps use too much gas anyway," he said. We took an exit off of 77 and ended up cruising into a string of residential districts. Somewhere along the way E had decided on a change of plans. We were heading some- dark where else. He told me there would be food there, so I didn't complain.

I wanted to tell him about Nick. I had almost let it out of the bag on the phone with him the first time I had called but something had stopped me. It was the same unknown thing that had me fiending for another cigarette so that I could exhale more smoke in the place of reality. But we both appeared to be out of cigarettes and I was never good at hiding anything from E.

"I killed a nigga!" I blurted out so fast that I don't think he really heard me.

"What the fuck are you talkin' about?" he said, laughing.

"That's why I'm here. 'Cause I killed a nigga."

He laughed harder this time. "Who the fuck did you kill?" he asked jokingly. I didn't say anything at first, and that somehow made him see that I was serious. The smile faded from his face. "Who the fuck did you kill?" he asked me again.

"You know Sierra, right?"

"You killed Sierra?" he asked in more of an alarmed tone than I'd ever heard him use.

"No. Shut up and let me finish. I walked in on her fucking some other dude over at her house."

"And you shot 'em both?"

"Nah, man. He ran the fuck out the house and I just stood there. And you know I had to tell Flake and Ray about that shit. So when I told 'em they was like we should go up to that nigga's job and do what we had to do. But we went up there and the cat ran out. We ran out after him and he started shootin' at us wit' a punk-ass .22. And he thought he got away but we seen him that night at a party for one of Snow's cousins who died. I ran up on him and we started boxin'. Then either Cuckoo or Ray put a .380 in my hand and when I chased him out back I just ended up shootin' him. I don't even remember decidin' do it. Next thing I knew I had pulled the trigger."

E didn't say a word for a while. I was surprised he hadn't pulled over or slammed on the brakes, but he just stared off into space. We finally came to a stop sign and he turned and looked at me.

"You sure you ain't fuckin' wit' me?" he said, making sure that I wasn't joking.

"How I'ma joke about killin' a nigga?"

He paused again and pulled a brand-new pack of Newports from the tray on the driver's-side door and handed me one. He took another for himself and lit us both up again.

"Well it's done now, nigga. Fuck it," he said, trying to convince his best friend that it was just something that had happened back at the neighborhood. But he knew what it meant. I'd now inadvertently crossed the line we'd drawn between us and Snow and Ray. "But you know you got a place to stay if you ain't ready to go home for a while. I know that place ain't the Ritz-Carlton or nothin', but it's a roof." Even if I was a murderer I was still his best friend.

E's reaction gave me the relief it had intended. I was still the same man. I'd just made a mistake. Sure it had cost someone his life, his family a loved one, Sierra a lover. But nonetheless it was a mistake. And mistakes could be forgiven.

"You ain't even got to say all that," I replied to his offer and pledge of allegiance. "The rules ain't changed." With that E grinned and he seemed comfortable again. He shifted the car back into drive and we finally pulled away from the stop sign.

We parked in front of a three-story house with a few people out in front of it. I'd confessed to an innocent party, and the complications of being a murderer hit me like a sledgehammer. My chest tightened and my feet started to tremble. I took a deep drag from my square and tried to relax. I breathed in and out and tried to look calm for my friend, the one who had accepted me even after knowing my crime. Just then I envied him. He'd gotten out in time.

"You glad you left, ain't you?" I asked.

"Right about now I most definitely am. I wish you had left wit' me." He sucked in the last half of his cigarette and flicked it out the window towards the street. A white cloud erupted from his nostrils, and he grinned to himself.

"What's so funny?" I asked.

"You," he said. "I gotta be honest. I ain't never figure you'd be able to do it. I know I couldn't have."

"Neither did I," I replied, remembering the bullet punching that hole through his frontal lobe, the bloody redness visible beneath the streetlight above. "You never know what you gonna do."

"Life's full of surprises, ain't it?" He took his key from the ignition. "Let's go." He ejected himself from the jeep, and I followed. The doors power-locked themselves behind us. E spoke to a few of the dudes outside before I followed him to the front door.

It was a thick oak door with a brass panther on the knocker. I hadn't even seen anything like it on TV. E brought it down twice with two loud thuds and I jettisoned the last of my cigarette towards the lawn. There was a long pause and I listened to a million crickets sing the same song from all sides of the house. But when the door finally opened the last thing I was thinking about was the crickets.

She was tall and slender like a track star. Her hair was a medium brown with blond streaks in it and her exposed stomach was rippled. She reminded me of that singer Aaliyah, but her lips had more of a pout to them. I didn't know who she was, but I was closer to love than I had ever been before.

"Took you long enough," she said with more of a southern accent than I had expected. She stood in the doorway without any sign that she planned to let us in.

"Sorry, baby, but I had to pick my boy up from his place over on Tryon. You know how out of the way that is," he said.

"I'll let you slide this time, but next time you won't be so lucky." She smiled. He wrapped his arm around her waist and pulled her into a kiss. It wasn't a short kiss, either. It was one of those kisses that you give your girl in public to let every man know that not only had the property been sold but so had all the land that was anywhere near it. My hopes with- dark
ered like a dream deferred. Then their lips released them.

"Oh I'm sorry, I'm Yvette." She reached out and shook my hand. "It's nice to meet you. What's your name?"

"That's my boy Thai," E said. For the first time in a long time I had actually wanted to answer myself.

"What, he can't speak?" she asked.

"Yeah, I can speak. He just like to hear himself talk," I replied.

"Ain't that the truth," she said, followed by the smile. "Come on in, sweetie."

It was a house straight off of the Cosby show. Cliff and Claire Huxtable were the only things that came to mind when I saw the books and the art and the spotless sofas and all the woodwork that surrounded us. Whoever Yvette's parents were, they were rich, and being rich was one more thing I knew nothing about.

Everyone was piled into the living room. There were at least twenty people, and all of them were wearing something that would have gotten them robbed where I was from. Most of the girls were on the rug sitting too close to the big-screen watching *Purple Rain.* I had never seen the movie before but I knew what it was. There weren't too many movies where a black man had on purple high-heel boots.

One of the girls on the floor was pregnant. Her round belly poked out of her Dolce and Gabbana T-shirt. She looked up at me but cut her eyes away before she thought that I could notice. The dudes sat on the couches behind the girls, or they stood in corners watching the girls watch the movie. A couple who looked a little older than the rest were snuggled up on the far couch in the corner. Two heavy-set girls came out of the kitchen with glasses of something clear that probably wasn't water. But there was someone in the background who really caught my attention.

She seemed tall for a girl, and when I saw her I forgot about my hunger. E tapped me on the shoulder and leaned over.

"Look before you touch," he said. It was a code that meant a lot of the girls had men and that they were the kind of dudes I shouldn't take lightly. Rich girls loved thugs. I nodded to him and then started across the sea of the uninteresting people towards the center of my attention. E was plotting to get Yvette upstairs. I envied him. Pussy was going to be a lot harder for me to come by.

As I moved towards my mystery woman I thought about E. He had changed. He wasn't the kid I had met on the basketball court who only had three pairs of pants, four shirts, and a pair of beat-up British Knights. But I wasn't the same either.

From the living room she had looked like a mannequin. Now she looked like a dancer, the kind from *The Nutcracker* or a musical. I saw *The Nutcracker* on a school trip. Her hips and shoulders were perfectly rounded, like a sculpture.

I didn't know what I was going to say as I approached. Looking around me I was definitely out of my element. That meant that she probably wasn't my cup of tea. But one had to try a different flavor now and again. I was sure that one of the usual tactics would suffice.

"What you doin' over here by yourself?"

"Mindin' my own business," she said without even looking at me. "You should do the same." Apparently the usual tactics weren't too effective. And of course I had my pride to consider.

"I am mindin' my own binness," I said. "You're blockin' my view."

"Your view of what?" she asked. She looked in my direction for the first time.

"The outside. You know? It's what you look through the window to see from the inside."

She smiled. That meant I had scored a point somewhere. "Yeah, I know that," she said, "but ain't nothin' out there but the dark."

"You don't like the dark?" I asked.

"Nah, 'cuz you can't see nothin'. Besides, people act crazy in the dark."

"People act crazy in the daytime too. Last week it was this dude on my block got high on angel dust and was running through the street with nothin' but his drawers on in the middle of the day," I said.

She laughed again, a little louder this time. I started to move closer, but then I hesitated.

"I ain't gonna bite you if you come over here," she said.

"I thought you would when you told me to mind my own binness. But anyway, I'm Thai."

"Well, I'm sorry, Thai. I'm just goin' through some things. I got a lot on my mind. Things hardly nobody know about."

"Everybody knows somethin'," I said. "When you add what you know with everybody else up in the world then you could say we know almost everything."

"But right now it's just you and me," she said, "and you can't help me."

"How do you know that? And what's your name?" I asked.

"My name's Alicia, and I'm just positive that you can't. You ain't got nothin' I can use."

"What you wanna bet?" I asked her.

"Whatever you want," she said. "I'm so sure I'll bet you whatever you want."

"If I'm right you gotta be my friend," I said.

"Is that all?"

"All the friends I got right now would take a bullet for me, so it ain't easy bein' my friend."

"I won't have to die for you tonight, will I?" she asked. She was serious.

"Nah," I said. "Hopefully you won't ever have to die for nobody."

"So what do I get if you can't help me?"

"My promise that I'll never try to holler at you again. I'll turn around and walk back to the livin' room and you won't ever have to be bothered."

"All right," she said, "but let's go out back. This is between me and you."

"Ain't nobody else here," I said.

I followed her slender shadow through the dining room and then the kitchen and then through a sliding screen door

that led to the back deck. We took a seat in two reclining chairs and looked into the darkness of the woods behind the house.

"So you ready to see if you can help me?" she asked playfully.

"Go 'head and hit me wit' it," I said.

A few rays of moonlight showed me her face in detail for the first time. Her chocolate face had slanted eyes like a Japanese cartoon, with thin lips and a wide nose. She was younger than I had thought, seventeen at the most.

"Do you know what it's like to kill something?" she asked.

I immediately switched to the defensive. Where was this question coming from? What did she know? Had the FBI been called in? Was I on the Most Wanted list for leaving the city? Maybe they already had Ray and Snowflake at the precinct as accessories. Maybe they were going to ship me up from Charlotte in a van just as soon as she had a confession on tape. There might have even been cops all in front of the building dressed undercover as teenagers. There was no way I was going to give in that easily.

"Nah," I said without hesitation.

"Well, I do," she said with a grave seriousness even an undercover cop couldn't feign. "I killed something important."

"I don't know what you mean," I said. "What you mean by something important?"

"I killed a person," she said. "Can you understand that?"

I was silent.

"Then I guess you better take your ass back in the living room and never speak to me again. Bye."

I didn't understand what she was saying or why she'd chosen me to hear her confession. What I had done with E in the car was necessary. He was my family. If I couldn't trust him I couldn't trust myself. But this girl, Alicia, only knew me as some cat that was trying to holler at her at a party. Didn't she know I could drop a dime, turn her in, and pick up ten Gs while dodging my own murder rap back in DC?

"Look, I ain't never killed nobody, but I got boys who have. I do know what it's like to need to get rid of something. Who'd *you* kill?"

She paused and then blurted it out at medium volume. "My baby. I killed it."

Her baby. She had killed her baby. I thought about my baby, the one that didn't make it to see the world. I pictured myself tearing her head off with my bare hands. I wanted to avenge the life she had somehow taken even though it had come out of her own womb. She was a killer in an entirely different way than I was. At least I had a reason. At least my victim had the chance to live a little of his life.

"Why the fuck you do that?"

"I got an abortion," she said, her words slurring slightly. "I ain't want no kid. I ain't want my kid to go through what it would've had to go through."

"And what was that?" I asked, now engrossed in the story. Something tightened inside of me as I listened.

"Its father. He would have killed it slowly. Sometimes I feel like bein' with him is killing me slowly." She said this nonchalantly. I wanted to comment but I was inundated by memory.

dark

4 1

One time I had to take Ray Ray's sister Tanya to get an abortion. She had got raped at a party out in Suitland by the Air Force base. And she got pregnant from it. I think that was the first man Snowflake had ever killed. At the time all I knew about abortion was that it was the way you got rid of a kid you didn't want. I didn't know how it was done. But while I was waiting for Tanya I asked the secretary and she told me. She told me that they stuck something up in the woman and scraped the baby out of the uterus and sucked it up in a vacuum tube. Alicia had gone through all of that because of the father. To me he had to be the worst thing on earth. But even that wasn't enough to make it right. It was her body, but it didn't make it right.

"Why are you telling me about this?" I asked.

"Because you said you could understand. And besides, you don't know me. You can't use it against me."

She was right about that, even though I wasn't going to tell her about Nick or why I was in Charlotte. But she was right. I couldn't hurt her. Even though I felt this pain knowing that my baby hadn't made it while she had practically thrown one away.

"How old are you?" I asked.

"Eighteen."

"You talk like you twenty-five," I said.

"People say I'm mature for my age."

"I guess," I said. I looked into the darkness with her. There was something there we were both still trying to find. I felt bad not telling her my tale. But I definitely couldn't afford to.

"Glad I never had a gun," she said, as if she'd pulled the truth from my mind. "I got a short temper and I got a lot of people I might pull the trigger on."

"Where'd that come from?" I asked.

"What?"

"The thing about the gun."

"Sometimes I think about shootin' him."

"Why don't you just break up with him?"

"My man ain't the type you just break up with. He can get crazy."

"Then you right. Be glad you never had a gun. Like they say on TV, havin' one make you wanna use it." I paused.

"I don't even wanna know your last name, Alicia," I said. "That way if you kill him I can never snitch."

She grinned. "T-H-A-I, like Thai food? What kind of name is that?" she asked.

"My dad said my mama liked Thai food. Thought it would be a cute name. Most people just think it's Tyrone."

"Your mother never told you herself."

"I never knew my mama," I replied. And the conversation continued.

Alicia had graduated from her high school in Brooklyn in June and moved to Charlotte in July. She had cousins at UNCC and she wanted to get away from where she grew up. Nearly a thousand miles south seemed to be just the right amount of distance. After an hour we had talked about everything from New York to DC and back again. I had won our little bet. Now she had to be my friend.

"You seem like you're real smart," she said.

dark

43

"I know enough to do what I gotta do," I said. "That's all that matters."

"You gonna go to college?" she asked. "I'm goin' to college."

"What you wanna go for?" I asked.

"I think I wanna be a physical trainer. You know, so I can help all the fine-ass athletes when they get hurt, plus I can get a little paid while I'm at it." She flashed another smile, the second since I'd met her.

"I hear dat," I said. "I'm trying to be in real estate, sell houses and buildings. Maybe I could buy some too. All I gotta do is live long enough and work hard enough."

She was the third person I had ever told this to. The first two were E and Pop. Pop had always wanted to go into real estate, and I wanted to go in with him. He knew the basics from books but he needed to take the classes so he'd know the rest and could be certified. But with his work schedule it was always hard to make the time, and when he had the time he said he didn't have the money. It was always something.

I wanted to go to school and get it started for him so that he could afford to make the time. But that meant that I had to get in school first.

"Everybody has dreams," she said. She had gone into the kitchen and stolen a carton of fruit punch from the fridge. We passed it back and forth like a forty-ounce. We had surprisingly ignored the plethora of liquor on the kitchen counter.

"But most people's don't ever come true. Shoot, I used to dream that I was gonna be a mad scientist and make Frankenstein monsters all day."

44

"I always wanted to be Batman," I said, " 'cuz Batman was just a regular dude but he was rich so he could make whatever he needed. He had a phat ride and a jet and a belt wit' a bunch of stuff on it. I made me a utility belt one time when I was eight. I made it out of one of my rope belts and some clothespins. I had a long string wit' a hook on the end and everything. But when I tried to climb this tree behind my boy's buildin' I fell and broke my arm. I had a cast on for most of that summer. And after that I stopped dreamin' about bein' Batman."

She laughed harder than I wanted her to, but it was funny. Besides, her laugh let me know she was actually human. We were drinking out of the same carton. Where I came from that was for people you had been down with from day one, and this was our first time together.

We stayed on the deck for ninety minutes before I even thought about the time. In those moments I imagined that she had grown up in the house next to mine, the boarded-up one that I used to play around until Pop told me it was condemned and made me stay away from it. She made me feel like I wasn't alone. I didn't want to be alone.

When she gave me her number I told her that I would call even though I knew it was best if I didn't. I had just gotten in town and she already knew too much.

"I gotta go and find my boy, but if I don't make it back here I'ma holler at you," I said.

"Call me tomorrow morning, 'cuz I work tomorrow night." She smiled and I gave her a hug before I went back into the house. I didn't want to leave her but I felt like I had to.

The crowd had thinned out in the living room. The pregnant girl, the couple, and the heavy-set twins had disappeared. *New Jack City* was on the big-screen and the girls had found guys. They were all nestled together as if they were all part of some cultist mating ritual. I walked past them to the foyer, where I hoped to find someone who would know where E might be.

I didn't want to look for him myself, because if I was with a girl like Yvette I wouldn't want anyone trying to find me until the rubber was off and I was on my way out the door. But I was in an unknown land where he was the only familiar thing. I decided to wait for him out on the front porch.

Most of the stragglers who we'd seen on the way in had gone as well. Three dudes were left on the porch. One was slumped over on the far edge passed out, and the other two were passing what was left of a blunt back and forth between them and staring out into the street. One of them saw me in the doorway and turned to me.

"You want a hit, dog?" he asked.

"Nah," I said. I never got drunk or high with people I didn't know. Ray Ray taught me that the first time he let me smoke.

"You don't smoke?" he asked, looking off somewhere to my right.

"They be random drug testin' at work so I can't even mess wit' it."

"Where you work at?" he asked.

"Department of Public Works," I said.

"Damn, I know the city don't be playin' wit' all that drug-testing shit. I'm glad I'm in school so I get to smoke a little longer."

"Yeah," I said.

"So how you know Yvette?" the other one asked.

"My boy E just brought me up here."

"You mean Enrique?" he asked.

"Yeah, that's my boy from home," I replied. He took another drag from the roach and shut up.

"Yeah man, I'm Chris. I'm Yvette's brother." He extended his hand and I slapped and locked it. "You ain't from here, is you?"

"Nah, man. I'm from DC," I said proudly.

"Shaw nigga!" E yelled from behind. He had never been much of a drinker, and I could tell he was a little buzzed. The smell of rum hanging in the air behind me proved it.

"You ready to roll?" he asked.

"Yeah, but I'll drive."

"You ain't got no choice," he said. "You gotta make sure I don't crash my shit."

"I guess we 'bout to roll," I said to Chris and the man with no name. The other dude was still slumped in the corner. E handed me the keys, and once I got situated in the driver's seat we took off.

I remembered the way we had come pretty well until we got off of the interstate. E showed me the way from there. I had wanted to ask where Yvette's parents were. I had also wanted to ask E about Alicia. But things were just beginning, dark

47

and I didn't want to know too many answers before the class even started. Pop had always told me that the truth was something you managed to gather along the way to wherever you were going.

We heard a loud yell from the top of the building on our way through the lobby, but we didn't investigate. It was close to three and I had been moving all day.

Apartment 3C was the way I had left it. No one had noticed that I'd been walking around with a 9mm tucked in my waistband. I tucked the gun underneath the sofa cushion after I walked in. E took the bed, but the sofa was softer. In my whole time there I never slept on the bed.

tuesday

"do you even know

what love is?" the shadow of a man asked me as he stood over me in that alley in Congress Heights. The barrel of a gun was right in my face and I couldn't speak. I could only hear his words repeatedly beating against my brain to the faint beat of the Backyard Band. But no matter how hard I thought about what he kept asking me I didn't get it. Then I woke up.

But the dream wasn't any worse than the reality of what I dark had to do. As I stood up and stepped into my sweatpants I wished that there was some way for me to do it without call-

49

ing. But of course there wasn't. And it was the only way to get any advance warning of what my fate might be. So I slipped my bare feet into my New Balances and pulled a T-shirt over head before I trotted down the three flights of steps to the lobby and then down Tryon to the pay phone on the corner. After I punched in my phone card number I imagined Snow's voice saying that they were already on their way to get me, that Nick's boys had driven up to the strip in front of Ray Ray's building and blasted everybody. Maybe he'd tell me that Pop had found out, thrown all my things out in the street and disowned me. But as the ringing stopped and the computerized voice kicked on I knew I wouldn't have to imagine much longer. I punched in the code to my voice mail only to find that I had no messages.

The laundry room in the basement was the perfect set for a horror movie. There was only one way in and one way out, and the stairwell was narrow. If you wanted to kill somebody that was the place to do it. But I was just there to wash my drawers, which I had forgotten to do during my two days of solitude.

I pulled my soggy boxers out of the washer in clumps and listened to the hum of my T-shirts on their final spin in the next machine. I hated that sound. That whizzing and whirring always made me think that the washer might explode and spit hot water and detergent in my face.

I had spent a lot of nights in Laundromats. Pop designated laundry as my first household duty when I was nine. I had to empty out both hampers, put the dirty clothes into garbage bags, and get them into the rusting metal grocery cart so that I could wheel them four blocks down the street to the Jiffy Laundromat.

Every step of the trip had to be done delicately. I had to pull the cart slowly. If one of those fifteen-pound bags fell over it was nearly impossible to get it back up without clothes spilling everywhere.

I did the laundry three times a month. The first time was just the regular run, but every other Thursday I made a special trip to do Pop's work shirts so he didn't have to do it on his one day off. On work-shirt Thursdays, Carla Bennett would be in there helping her grandmother wash. Carla was fifteen and she was one of the first girls I ever really wanted to get with. I had daydreams of dragging my skinny ten-year-old frame right over to her and asking her out, but I'd always come to the firm conclusion that I was ten and she was fifteen and that was a hurdle I couldn't get over.

Carla's mama was white and she worked as an orderly at Howard Hospital up the street. I'd see her after school sometimes, but I only saw Carla on those Thursdays. We'd talk for two or three minutes about absolutely nothing and then I'd go to my washer and she'd go back to helping her grandmother and that was it. We weren't even friends, but she kept me from being by myself. I was an only child who had to be home by the time the streetlights came on, so anyone who kept me company was good enough.

I was so busy thinking about Carla Bennett that I didn't even notice my new laundry room companion as she walked in.

"Hope you don't mind a little company?" she said as she broke the silence.

I turned my head to see the eighth wonder of the world. She knew what I was looking at, a Coca-Cola bottle in uniform.

"Nah," I said. "Not at all."

"You gotta be new," she said, grinning. "I ain't seen you before." Her voice was missing that Charlotte quality Yvette's had overemphasized.

"You could say that," I replied as I twisted my body around to face her. "I just got here."

"From where?" she asked curiously. She was wearing a dark blue flight attendant uniform with pantyhose and a fresh pair of Adidas Galaxies. It was an odd combination.

"Someplace you wouldn't want to go to," I said.

"I'm a flight attendant. Ain't nothin' I ain't seen. I go everywhere."

"I'm from DC," I said.

"All right. Now that I know I promise I won't make any jokes about your mayor smokin' crack if you don't start telling me how boring it is down here."

"Whatever," I said.

"You just look like you'd rather be somewhere else," she said.

The way she looked at me made me uncomfortable. She had devilish eyes, the kind of eyes you couldn't trust with anything, and she was using them to size me up. She stood right in front of me as she loaded her clothes into the washer. I could see the perfect curves in her thighs.

"What's your name?" I asked.

"Robin." She extended her free hand and I shook it. "What's yours?"

"Thai," I said.

"Like Tyrone."

"No, like Thailand."

"Oh, that's pretty interesting. Who gave you that name?"

"My mama."

"She never told you why?"

"My father said she liked Thai food, thought it would be cute. But I never met her," I said, "so there's a lot she ain't told me."

"I'm sorry," she said. She was older than me. Maybe twenty-two or twenty-three.

"What you sorry for? Like they say: You can't miss what you never had."

"I guess," she said. She added detergent to the load. I looked at my watch. It was almost nine. I had slept through most of the day and wasted the rest.

"So what brings you to Charlotte?" she asked.

"Just came down to see my best friend from home. He moved down here about a year ago. That's my story. Now tell me about you?"

"Well," she said in a fake California valley girl voice, "I'm twenty-three and I work for Delta Airlines and I like working out, dancing, and meeting men in the laundry room of my building."

"You got a little comedian in you," I said.

"That along with everything else," she replied. There was

something in the way she finished the sentence that started an erection that didn't stop. She was hungry for something and I wanted to feed it to her.

In less than ten minutes she'd plopped herself on the bench next to me and I learned that she was from Oakland and she had come to Charlotte to take care of an aunt who had since passed away. Heart disease. Now she worked for Delta. She'd been in the building for about six months and said it was the kind of place where you rarely saw anybody unless you sat on the stoop and watched them come in and out. My load had long since finished, but I didn't want to pull away from her.

"So how old are you?" she asked me. I could tell that she didn't have a clue. Most people didn't. With the beard and the nappy 'fro I could have been anywhere from sixteen to twenty-six.

"How old do you think I am?" I asked.

"I don't know. That's why I'm asking." She moved closer. Her legs couldn't have been two inches away from mine on the bench. I could hear her every exhale as it hit the air.

"I'll keep it to myself," I said.

"And why is that?"

"Because I don't want you to discriminate."

"Can you vote, drink, and drive?"

"Yeah." I had a fake ID, so how much of a lie was the drinking part?

"Well, that's all that matters then."

"Yeah, I guess you right. So you really don't need to know," I said.

She had one of those cute-little-girl-who-grew-up-too-fast kind of faces, an angel with a rap sheet longer than her wings. She didn't cross her legs, but held them together like she was sitting under a table. I wanted to split them apart.

She told me about the city and what there was to do there. There was an amusement park called Carowinds, a twenty-screen movie theater off of Interstate 77, cosmic bowling, laser tag, one small black history museum, a few clubs, and the occasional decent stage play. She told me her airline was hiring if I needed a job and there was a bar down the street called Esperanza that had really good sandwiches.

The clock on the wall read ten-thirty. Carla Bennett and I hadn't said nearly as much and we had done laundry together for two years all the way up to when she moved to North Carolina when I was in the seventh grade.

"Damn, I gotta get back upstairs and start folding," I said. "We should kick it, though. Maybe do somethin' sometime."

"Yeah," she said softly. "I'm in 3F."

"For real? I'm in 3C."

"3C?" she asked as if to make sure.

"Yeah."

"Maybe I'll come by and holler at you," she said.

"Whatever you want to do," I said.

I turned and headed up the stairs toward the elevator. But she was twenty-three and even though she hadn't said it she probably had a man who was paying her rent and enjoying her whenever she wasn't flying the friendly skies. Fine girls always had men and their man was always some chump

dark

whom you looked at and wondered what he had that you didn't.

In high school Ray Ray and I used to stand outside the Ritz on Sundays and see the girls with their carbon-copy men all the time. The girls would always look at us like they knew we were broke.

"Fuck them stuck-up bitches!" Ray Ray would yell after one would walk past. It was usually the one he thought was the finest.

I just watched and took mental notes and waited for the moment when I'd be a contender. Once I got my degree and went into real estate with Pop everything was gonna be all right. Then the girls would have to take a number.

I sat my laundry down and turned on the TV. An episode of *Vegas* was on one of the three UHF stations that came through clearly. No cable. The phone number Alicia had given me the night before was on the nightstand next to the bed but I'd forgotten I didn't have a phone. Besides, it had only been twenty-four hours so it was too soon to call. I thought about paging E from the phone on the corner, but I figured that if he was as whipped as he seemed then he was out at Yvette's doing what needed to be done.

The Beretta was laid across the wood coffee table like a corpse on a slab. I picked it up and studied it in the flickering light from the TV. It was still on safety. I set it back down and then I picked it up again and tucked it back under the sofa.

On the couch I waffled between wanting to sleep and staying awake. But my body curled up like an infant's and I listened to the Barney Miller theme song on TV until I couldn't hear it anymore.

"Brrrrrrrring!" the doorbell screamed at me. I jumped to attention only to see the snow falling down on itself across the TV screen. My watch glowed 2:00 A.M. My neck was stiff but I got to my feet and measured each step towards the door. My mind was somewhere between DC and Charlotte when I flung the door open. I didn't think about the peephole. It was Robin.

"I gotta ask you something," she said.

"Sure, come on—"

"No. I gotta ask you right now."

"What?" I rubbed the corners of my eyes but I didn't feel any sleep there.

"Is it wrong to want something even when you might not deserve it?"

"Like what?" I asked. She was wearing sweatpants and an old Oakland Raiders T-shirt. No socks. Her toenails were painted a bright green.

"What if I said I wanted you to kiss me?"

"I wouldn't say anything. I'd probably just do it."

"Then do it."

Up until that moment I was pretty sure that women only behaved that way on late-night TV or when you had a platinum album and a Lexus to go with whatever you were saying. And while I definitely had my appeal with the ladies I wasn't Denzel standing there in sweat shorts and a Fila T-shirt. But I didn't have anything to lose. So I kissed her, with semi-morning breath. She dissolved into my mouth and

dark

my chest and everything else. I slid my hands across her derrière and gripped it tightly. That was when she stopped and pushed me away.

"Thank you," she said. "Sleep tight."

She turned and walked back down the hall to the open doorway that led to her apartment and closed the door behind her. I just stood there halfway out of my door and tasted the minty mouthwash that had coated her tongue. Charlotte girls were strange.

Now imagine being me: nineteen, stressed as hell over the possibility of getting locked up on murder one, standing in my doorway with a hard dick and just having been tongued down by one of the finest girls I'd ever met in my life. She was playing a game I didn't know the rules to. I was still half asleep and the last thing I wanted was a nice attempted rape charge for knocking on her door at two in the morning. But I figured that I could always run to the car and head out of town if things didn't go my way.

Each step down that hallway made me feel a year younger, and by the time I was in front of 3F I felt like I was in the fifth grade trying to ask Carla Bennett for her phone number. I raised my hand to knock but I stopped myself. I tried again but the same thing happened. The third time I tapped it and the door gave way. It wasn't even closed all the way. I just hoped that there wasn't some hit-man boyfriend on the other side of the door that I might have to pop with the piece I had stashed back in 3C.

"Robin?" I said into the crack in the door.

"It's two in the morning," her voice said.

"I didn't tell you that when you came to my door."

"You and me ain't the same person," her voice replied.

"I gotta ask you a question."

"Then open the door and ask."

Her voice wasn't the same as it had been in the laundry room. Its tone was lower and more to the point. I liked it better the new way. I pushed the door open and saw her standing in the middle of the efficiency with nothing on but her sweatpants.

"Why me?" I asked, sounding confused.

" 'Cuz you were in the right place at the right time," she said.

"So this is just gonna work for right now?" I asked.

"You have to impress me to make me think about tomorrow."

"Ain't you gotta go to work?"

"I'm off," she said. I didn't say anything else.

I walked up to her and kissed her again, completing what I had started in my doorway. Her bare breasts pressed against my T-shirt. I massaged her booty and she ran her cool hands up my back. I shuddered but I kept on kissing. My hands developed a mind of their own as they cupped her breasts and nipples. I slid her sweatpants off and came out of everything I had on.

She gave me a condom. I wanted her to remember me in the morning. She leaned against the arm of the sofa while I entered from the back. I gave it everything I had as I went in and out of her. I think I did a pretty good job. But I won't lie. She worked me.

dark

Beams of sunlight burst into her apartment hours later. As my eyes focused I could see her sitting at the computer on the other side of the room. I needed glasses but I never got any. Glasses wouldn't look right on a five-eleven skinny dude.

"You got up this early on your day off?" I asked.

"I'm writing a letter to my mama," she said. She had on a different T-shirt with the same sweatpants from the night before.

"But it's like seven in the morning."

"It's almost eight. Usually when I fly I get up at four."

A pair of grandma spectacles sat across her nose, and her hair was a mess. That had partly been my fault. She finished the letter, saved it, and turned the computer off while I was still getting it together.

"You ain't gonna mail it?" I asked. She got up and came back over to the bed and sat down next to me.

"I never mail them," she said. "They're not for her to read now."

"What you mean?" I asked.

"I'm just going through this period in my life that I think my mama should know about. But I don't want her to know while the things are happening. She'd be down here with a shrink and a preacher at the same time."

"So what's this period in your life about?" I asked.

"Me," she said. "Giving me what I want and not letting anything get in my way."

"Is that what last night was about?" I asked.

"Pretty much," she said coolly. "The old me would have seen you, gone home, and played with myself thinking about what could have happened."

"Damn," I said with my dark skin finding a way to blush. "I guess you just don't give a fuck."

"You wouldn't understand."

"Well, explain it to me. I know you got the time if it's your day off. You hungry?"

"Yeah, I could go for something," she said, moving her head towards my dick but lifting it again and smiling.

"Is it like a pancake house or somethin' around here?"

"It ain't too far away," she replied.

"Well then, let me buy you breakfast," I said while looking around the bed for my T-shirt.

"All right," she said.

It took us twenty minutes to get to the IHOP on Independence Boulevard and another fifteen for a table. People were in there with their families and their parents like it was Sunday after church. Robin still wore her grandma glasses with the same T-shirt and sweatpants but she now wore a Polo baseball cap over her mangled mane.

A white lady with about sixteen chins sat us down in a tiny window booth at the back of the restaurant next to four white businessmen and their coffeepot. Robin sat across from me and gave me a look more intense than any of her previous stares.

"So what is it you want from me, Thai?" she asked.

"Why I gotta want somethin'?" I stuck my eyes to the menu. The two-egg breakfast looked good.

"You're a man. Men always want something. That's what makes them men."

"Then what does that make y'all women?"

"We're the reason why you always want something because you want to give us something so we'll let you get us."

"I don't think I'm hearin' you," I said, confused.

"Think about it. What are some of the things you do the most to get a woman's attention? You do something that gets you noticed. You have something to get noticed. You make them notice you. That's what y'all live for."

"All right. I hear you so far," I said.

"Don't you see that in the history of the world, men have done all that they've done to gain something to get noticed, to achieve something to get noticed, or to make the world notice something about them?"

"I guess I see what you're sayin'."

"For most of y'all there ain't no fun in havin' nothin' or bein' nothin' if you can't have and be with somethin' else that snuggles up to you at night."

"Don't y'all need that too?" I asked.

"Women always need and want more than the perfect man could give them. At least I do."

"You sound like you've got your mind made up."

"Experience is the best teacher," she said.

"I learned a lot from you last night," I replied, trying to get away from any intellectual discussion. The devilish look returned to the caramel eyes that matched her skin tone.

"But the bottom line is this: If you brought me here because you want me, I'll tell you now that you can't have me.

I'm not lookin' for no relationships or no boyfriends or nothin'."

"Hey look, I'm only down here for a little while anyway. I don't want nothin' from you that you don't wanna give me. To be real wit' you I can't really give you much more than this either. I got too much goin' on myself."

"Just as long as we have an understanding," she said.

"Whatever you want," I replied.

We ordered. I could tell she was still sleepy, because her eyes were narrow behind her glasses and the yawns came in five-minute intervals. I told myself that she wasn't used to getting up at six after a night with me.

"So what's up with this period in your life you got to write letters about?" I asked right after the food came. She lit a cigarette even though we were in the nonsmoking section and took a deep drag. She exhaled a thin spiral of smoke that danced its way up toward the ceiling.

"I was hoping you'd forget to ask," she said, grinning. Her full lips looked like they stuck to her teeth when she smiled.

"I got a good memory. So you gonna tell me or not?" I asked.

"What you wanna know for? You probably already think I'm a hoe."

"No I don't. I didn't expect last night. To be honest I don't know what you are. That's why I'm buying you breakfast and askin' all of these questions."

"What are you, nineteen? Twenty?"

"What?" I asked.

"That's how old you are," she replied.

"What makes you say that?"

"It's something in the way you fuck." My dark skin blushed again. "You can tell a lot about somebody by how they are in bed."

"What do you mean?"

"It's like you know what you're doing but you haven't known it for too long, because at points you go back over the basics just in case you forgot something. I think I was like that when I was nineteen or twenty. So that's my guess."

"I'm nineteen," I said. Then I brought us back to the subject at hand. "Now tell me about this period in your life."

"You ain't givin' up on that, are you?" she said. Her cigarette had burned to a butt. "Well, like I told you, I came down here to take care of my aunt 'cause she had heart disease and diabetes and she had been in and out of the hospital because she wasn't taking her medicine. She was my favorite aunt and things weren't too good with me and my mama, so I came out here to take care of her for a while. But the minute I got here it seemed like she got worse and the worse she got the more helpless I felt for not being able to do more for her. And for those couple of months that turned out to be her last I ate, drank, and slept her. I never went out to the club or to get my hair done or nothin'. In fact, that's why I actually cut my hair off. But when she died I realized that even though God had took her home at seventy she had lived her life the way she wanted. And she had died knowing that. And after the funeral when I thought about it I was like 'I'm twenty-three and I ain't done nothin'.' I ain't been nowhere. I didn't even go to college. It was like I'd spent all the time since high school just taking up space in the world. And I was like, I need to start doin' what I want to do every day. So I got this little flight attendant job and I get to go everywhere and I get to do what I want and last night I wanted you."

"Why me?" I asked. I was stuck in a trance reliving the highlights from the night before.

"First, it was because you were there and you were cute. Second, it seemed like you were trying really hard not to let me know how much you wanted me. And I guess that turned me on."

"Well, I do my best," I said.

"I know you do. I want to see what you'll be like in a year or two, what kind of man you'll be."

"So when does this period in your life end? When you gonna stop just doin' what you want to do?"

The expression on her face went from plain to sad and she started looking out the window. She had let me into the room that led to the room where she kept all of her secrets. But that was as far as I was allowed. And it wasn't just about her aunt. Somebody had done something to her behind that locked door she only allowed me to stand in front of. I knew that I might never know what it was.

"I don't really know," she said. "I don't know."

"What about love?" I asked.

"What about it?" she said, still looking out the window.

"You ever had it?"

"Too much of it, not enough of it. Had it all and I don't feel like bein' bothered with it right about now. Love is like your favorite cousin from out of town. When it's there you love it and have all the fun you can with it but when it's gone you're just left with the memories and empty space it leaves you until the next time."

"You talk like you forty," I said.

"Forty ain't that far away," she said.

"I ain't never been in love, so I wouldn't know," I said.

"You will," she replied, "and it'll happen when you need it least. It always does. That's why I'm not even trying to be bothered with it anymore."

She dropped me off in front of the building a little before ten. She had some errands to run and then an early flight the next morning. I didn't know what it was I felt about her just then. She was right. Part of me wanted the something from her that she couldn't give me. Even though I didn't know her last name I wanted into that secret room so I could figure out what she was afraid of and why she didn't want to get too close to me.

I watched her car disappear down Tryon. I wondered if I would spend the night at her place again or if our breakfast after had been it. Then I stopped thinking about it altogether. I had bigger problems to deal with.

a mother
and son

"so when's mama comin' home?"
Raj had asked Dee on the episode of *What's Happenin'* I had
watched before laundry the night before. If I had been Dee I
wouldn't have known the answer. For me my mama was a
blob of nothingness like the shadow in my dream, an empty
word from the time I was born. At nineteen she took up
enough space to have her own room inside my brain and the
bigger she got the more questions she left that I didn't have
the answers to. All I knew was that she was from Baltimore
and that they'd cut me out of her stomach because her hips

were too narrow, and that her name was Delilah. That was it. No pictures. No nothing.

Every time I asked Pop about her he'd tell me that I didn't want to know. Then within ten minutes he'd walk the two blocks up to the liquor store across from the Shaw train station and buy a fifth of gin to drown whatever information he might have had before it got out of his throat. I had tried more than ten times in nineteen years and they all met with the same result.

Most people I knew had it the other way around. Their father was that blob of empty space. But to me that was easier because there were all kinds of people in the world with no fathers. Those people always had someone else to identify with. The only person who came close was E. But his mama came back so he couldn't understand anymore either.

I had a million theories on why she wasn't around. When I first met Snowflake he tried to convince me that Pop might have killed her and buried her under the house. Then I thought that maybe she got hit by a car and got amnesia and was out there trying to find out who she was. Maybe she had been abducted by aliens or was in the witness protection program. But by the time I hit high school I assumed that she was some junkie or tramp who had caught a better train and left Pop holding the bag with me inside of it.

I moved on without her. Nothing kissed my bumps and bruises besides Q-Tips and peroxide. I wiped my own face in the morning and taught myself to never show any weakness. If you got hurt you shook it off. If someone said something about me I had to come back with something better. When people died it was messed up but that was the risk you ran for living. Girls were an alien race who you entered and left, unless you loved them or gave them your baby. That was the way I lived.

But for some reason Mama hung heavy on my mind as I climbed the stairs towards Apartment 3C. The door was cracked when I got there and my first impulse was that I'd gotten robbed on my third day in Charlotte. But as I pushed the door open and saw E in another fresh shirt and tie watching TV I laughed at my paranoia.

"Where your ass been all morning?" he asked, looking up. "I been here for two hours. A nigga got things to do, you know?"

"Don't act like you couldn't call and see if I was here."

"You ain't got no phone!" he said, laughing. I had forgotten again.

"So wassup?" I asked.

"Moms wants me to bring you down to the office," he said as if it was serious business.

"What for?" I asked cautiously.

"To turn you in to the cops. Stop being a little bitch. She just wants to say hi. She ain't seen you in a year."

It wasn't like E's mama and I had ever been close. I was sure that we had never said more than three words to each other at one time. I'd only seen her twice in my life, so all this "bring Thai down to the office for old time sake" stuff was news to me. Besides, his mom was Indian and all the other Indians I'd ever seen were the ones who kept their hands on the shotgun behind the bulletproof glass when I wanted five

dark

6 9

on pump number three. How had she ended up with Mr. Mitchell anyway? Aside from all of that I was preoccupied with the idea of sticking around until Robin came back.

"I ain't gettin' dressed up," I said. I didn't have anything to get dressed up in.

"Ain't nobody ask you to get dressed up. We gon' run down here for a while and I'll bring you back."

"All right," I said. "But let me hit the shower first."

"Whatever, just don't take all day," he replied, turning his attention back to the TV.

for the second day in a row

I nervously checked my messages, this time from E's cellular. But once again I found nothing. Where was Snow and why didn't he have anything to tell me? Didn't he know that he was my only link to my fate? Didn't he know he was the only person who could save me from feeling like life as I knew it was about to end? For someone else an absence of news might have been calming. But for me it was just more stress. As we rode along I looked away at the sight of passing police cars and compulsively reminded E twice that he was driving over the speed limit. I needed to hear something from someone. But E's mama wasn't exactly who I had in mind.

The real estate office wasn't too far from the IHOP I had just come from. It was a converted two-story house at the end of a little tree-lined street off of Independence Boulevard.

"Coming down here might have saved my life," E said

when we were two minutes away from the office. "I ain't really know if there was anything past DC," he said. "So if you end up wantin' to stay, I can see if I can work something out with Moms about the apartment."

"Thanks, man, but I don't know about stayin'. I'm just here until I know for sure if the cops is lookin' for me or if they isn't. If they ain't knockin' on my door I can go back, maybe risk getting shot by somebody's crew for shootin' their boy. If they is lookin' for me then you won't see me again until I got gray hair."

"You ain't goin' out like that, man. Even if we gotta get you to Mexico you ain't goin' out like that. But forget about all that. I'm just saying that if you want to come down here you can."

But even if I wasn't a murderer on the run, could I just up and leave Shaw? I pictured Pop lying on the couch in the living room like he always did when I left for work. I wondered if he would miss me if I never came back. I hadn't even thought about staying in Charlotte. What would there be for me to do in a makeshift city that didn't feel anything like home? But I had to ask myself what ultra-important things I was doing at home. Move to Charlotte? It wasn't likely, but anything was possible.

"Well, I'll let you know," I replied. In my mind I was measuring the length of my jail cell and trying to figure out how long it would take for me to make my first shank inside. Not hearing from Ray and Snow wasn't good. It wasn't good dark at all.

The office was ice-cold, perfect in contrast to the heat

right outside of its doors. There was a receptionist at the front and then there were two offices behind her. E pointed out the smaller one as his office and the larger as the room where they kept all the forms and supplies. His mom's office was all the way at the back, and it had a closed door with a little knocker on it. As we approached I imagined opening that door to see a skinny little Indian woman in traditional clothes smoking a big cigar with her feet on the desk, and I grinned to myself. E tapped on the door. I looked down and noticed that the carpet was a bright red and that it didn't go with anything else in the office.

"It came with the place," E said while shaking his head at the color himself. I nodded to him just as the door opened.

When she opened the door she didn't look any different from the first time I'd seen her except she had on a business suit and her hair was pinned up. She smiled at me like she might at a long-lost nephew.

"How you doin' boy?" she said the way a black woman would but with an Indian accent. On the way over E had mentioned that his mama had spent three of her four years in college rooming in a black dorm with a roommate from somewhere in Mississippi. But it still surprised me. I tried not to laugh and hurt her feelings.

"I'm all right, Ms.—"

"Mehdi. I know you don't know my name."

"You right about that," I said, forcing a smile.

"So is the apartment okay?" She motioned both of us in.

"It's fine," I said. "Thank you very much for hookin' me up. I really needed to get out for a while."

"Everyone gets like that sometimes," she said. "I know Enrique was like that." E gave me a look of affirmation.

"So is your business going good?" I asked.

"We're doing fine for a small company just starting out. We only have four properties, the one where you're staying and three others near Smith College. We also sell homes as well. So as long as everyone gets paid I don't think we'll have too many complaints."

"I hear that," I replied.

She had fallen into the real estate game when an old employer of hers had left her one of his buildings when he died. She sold it and used the money from the sale to buy four more with only a little money down. The money she got from rent was more than enough to pay her mortgages, her salary, and her employees. That wasn't bad for a little Indian woman who still had trouble saying words with a long *o* in them.

I looked around her office. It was relatively small compared to most offices I had seen. There were two shelves filled with all kinds of books. A piece of woven fabric was stretched across a wood frame that hung on the wall, and there was a professional photograph of her and E on her desk next to her laptop. There was also a small file drawer in the corner.

"So how's your family?" she asked cheerfully.

"Pop is doing okay. He wants to sell real estate too some-day."

"Really?" she said. "He should go ahead and take the classes. They're only one or two nights a week."

"He's the kind of person who's gonna do it when he gets ready," I said.

"I definitely know a lot of people like him," she replied. "I actually went without the classes when I first started, but I made some mistakes." And then the phone rang.

"Sorry boys, but I've got to get back to work. Maybe you'll come to church with us Sunday." That same roommate had also converted her into a Baptist.

"Maybe," I said, trying to be polite but knowing that I was more than unlikely to go to church.

We closed her door behind us and went into E's office. It was even smaller than his mom's and the desk was covered with mail and Post-it notes to the point where you couldn't even see the desktop.

"You can't keep nothin' clean," I said.

"Fuck you, all right?" he replied. He got on the phone and called Yvette and told her something like we'd be coming by to see her at the mall. I felt like reminding him that he'd said he'd have me back at the apartment, but I let it go.

"So what's up with you and Yvette? I know you ain't just got one girl down here," I asked on our way to the mall. I rolled down the window and watched the smoke from my cigarette get sucked into the wind.

As fine as she is, you think I'ma let one of these weak niggas down here lock her down before me? Besides, Yvette is all I need."

"Where'd you meet her, anyway?"

"You gon' laugh if I tell you," he said as he kept his eyes on the road. He was playing the *Superfly* sound track in the deck.

"I ain't gon' laugh as long as you gettin the ass."

"Well then you definitely gon' have a straight face on. I met her at a cocktail party."

"At a *what?*"

"It like a little party where everybody walks around—"

"I know what it is. But you from Shaw. Shaw niggas don't be goin' to no cocktail parties."

"You know, T, it's a whole world past the neighborhood."

"What are you talkin' about? You know, that's the second time you said that since yesterday."

He took a sharp left and turned to me when he stopped at a red light. "Let me ask you sumpin'. How many times you been up by UDC since I left?"

UDC was where I was supposed to go to school, the city college where the mayor promised admission to any public high school graduate and they could go for free. I had the admission packet but I had yet to fill it out. Sometimes I went up there to stare at the buildings and imagine what it would be like to be in college.

"I don't know," I said, thinking hard about it. "Maybe a few times. You know I don't be up that way a lot."

"Why don't you be up there?" he asked.

"Because that ain't where I'm from. It ain't like I'm in college up there yet."

"Tell me three streets up that way besides Van Ness and Connecticut Avenue. Tell me one place you know is up there that ain't near a train station."

"Why I need to know that? I don't live up there."

"So what you sayin' is that you lived in DC all your life

dark

and you ain't been around the whole city enough to know more than a couple of streets uptown. DC ain't really even a big city and I bet you ain't even been through half of it."

"I ain't followin' you."

"See, when I came down here I was just tryin' to see what it was like somewhere else. And it's a lot of things I hate about Charlotte. But down here I got a job in a office workin' for my mama. Ain't no government layoffs or somebody I know gettin' shot every other month. I make twelve dollars an hour and I ain't got no rent or no bills to pay. Down here I think I got a better chance."

He had changed. Now he wore suits and khakis and was messing with girls who lived in townhouses in the suburbs. That wasn't the E I knew. He talked like him, maybe even thought like him, but he just wasn't the same. I had to come to terms with the fact that a year had made a difference. He was so far out of the loop that to him Congress Heights could have been Cancún. He wanted me to get out and see the rest of DC. I didn't need to. I had seen all that I needed to see in and around my way. I went to work and came home. I knew where to get something to eat and where to go to the movies. I knew the malls. I even knew where the museums were. So what was there to see in those unfamiliar places? How was that going to make me a better person? I was making it and surviving. Pop and I had a house and decent jobs, and Snowflake and Ray Ray were all right. I had moved on without E. I had made it despite everything I didn't have.

"You glad you got a mama?" I asked. I didn't know

where the question came from, but it had obviously been there since we'd gotten into the car.

"What you mean?" he asked.

"You know what I mean," I said, turning the volume down on the radio. "When we was in the fifth grade you asked me how come you never saw my mama and I told you 'cause *I* ain't never seen her, and you said you ain't never seen yours either. I mean, what's that like? You get to live wit' her and everything."

"Yeah, I ain't never think it was gonna happen," he said, almost sadly. "For a long time I hated her for not bein' there. But she came back and she saved my life."

"Saved your life? What she save you from? You thought you was gonna die or somethin'? You was all right. We was always gonna make sure you was all right."

"I know y'all had my back, but I still used to think about it a lot. Especially that last year of school," he said reflectively. "If me and you had just ended up in the wrong place one more time, you know bullets can only miss for so long."

"Man, we nineteen. If we ain't got shot by now we gonna be all right."

"What's all right, though? Do you really wanna be filing papers downtown at Public Works forever?" he asked me.

"Nah."

"But why you do it?"

" 'Cuz it pay good money. Ten dollars a hour. That's all right for me right now. I get my yearly evaluation in a couple dark weeks, get a raise. In about three or four years I might be makin' thirty-five Gs a year," I said.

"But is that really what you wanna do? I know it's at least two days out the week when you think about not wanting to go in. What do you *really* wanna do?"

I paused for a moment. Three days out of five I wanted to be somewhere else, even if it was just on the corner with the rest of the boys.

"Well, you know I wanna help Pop do his real estate thing like you got wit' your moms. Have a little father-son thing or somethin'."

"How you gon' do that workin' down at Public Works?"

"I got some money saved up."

"When you gon' go to school or get your license or see about working at a real estate company, something to get you started on how it works?"

He sounded like my tenth-grade English teacher, and it made me feel funny, almost the way I felt when I walked into Sierra's house and found Nick fucking her on the floor in front of the TV. They were two different situations but they felt the same. Nick had taken it too far. E had too much to say and it made too much sense. There was no room to argue, only space to embrace the truth, truth that had pressed itself against my temple and made me react. It had made me grip that .380, and as E's words shook my skull I thought of the 9mm that was under my sofa. I just wanted him to shut up. I turned my head towards the window so I didn't have to watch his lips move.

He knew what I had risked by shooting Nick. He knew that there was a fifty-fifty chance that the next time he saw me would be behind Plexiglas or in a casket. But for the sake of being everything Snow wasn't, E wanted me to see that there was a chance the grass could still be green on my side of the fence. But I didn't want to open my eyes.

"Shit. I ain't got nobody to save me."

He gave me a look harder than steel and then let out a deep sigh.

"Don't even go dere," he said calmly. "My moms gave me a chance. That's all. She ain't holding my hand and wipin' my nose for me."

"Yeah, but she left you and your dad too."

"Yeah, she did," he said matter-of-factly.

"And your ass wasn't mad that she left you for twelve years? She got up and walked out your house wit' your ass playin' on the livin' room floor and you don't wanna smack her for just trying to show up and be your mama like shit is all cool?"

"How I'ma hate my mama when she brought me in the world? How I'ma hate her for doing what she had to do?" He sighed. "But this ain't about my mama. It ain't even about your mama. You stuck between a rock and a hard place and you ain't got nothin' else to do but start fightin' with the one nigga you shouldn't be."

Just then he was the old E again. He was the one who took the bottle out my hand after I smashed it over this dude's head so I wouldn't cut his throat the night before graduation. E had pulled me through the basement window of a house party on Valentine's Day when two dudes started shooting at

dark

each other inside over the pregnant girl they shared. E knew me, maybe even better than I knew myself.

"You right, man," I said softly. "My fault. I'm sorry."

"Yeah," he said calmly. The tension relaxed and he turned the radio back up and kept his eyes on the road.

Three minutes later the mall came into view. I didn't feel like seeing Yvette or anyone who might have been with her. As long as I was in Charlotte I was a walking candidate to be set up with every single girl Yvette knew. I wasn't ready for all of that, not until I had called Alicia at least once. She had been at the party, so she at least knew Yvette, and the worst thing that could happen was to get set up with two different girls and they turn out to know each other. That had happened to Ray Ray once.

A girl named Bridgette who had lived in his building had set him up with her cousin Keisha one day. Two weeks later he fucked her and sent her on her merry way. Then about a month later Bridgette hooked him up with her sister's best friend, who had taken some dude from Keisha earlier in the year. It ended up in a boxing match between Ray Ray, Keisha's new boyfriend, and the two girls in the food court at Union Station on a Sunday. Ray cracked the dude's ribs with a food court stool before security showed up. He spent three hours in the security office before they let him go and told him he was banned from the premises. But he still came back the next week.

You always had to make sure that all of the bases were covered. If loose ends meant the wrong thing to the wrong person you got a beatdown over the he said/she said. It was all stupid. But that was how it was. I saw why E was glad to be out.

"Now this is the mall where all the high school kids come to," E said as he parked the jeep right in front of the entrance.

It was called Eastland Mall and from the looks of things it was where you went when there was nothing else to do. I didn't recognize the names of a lot of the stores, but malls are malls. The faces behind the counters were mostly the same age as those in front, and I felt like I was older than all of them. I wasn't in high school anymore and it made me feel older than I ever had.

Once I started working for Public Works I didn't see too many people my age unless I was on the train, at the playground, or at Ray Ray's. Down in Charlotte they all looked even younger.

"All these broads is young as hell," I said, looking around.

"And they get younger," E replied as we approached Yvette's booth, "but most dudes down here really don't give a fuck about how young girls are. I seen thirty-five-year-old dudes wit' fourteen-year-old girls."

"That's a damn shame. I wasn't never big on gettin' no young girls," I said.

"Now you see why I got a girl two years older than me," E said.

"I guess," I replied, thinking that Yvette didn't look that much older than us.

She worked at one of the many carts in the marketplace in the middle of the second level of the mall. Her cart displayed a large selection of silver jewelry. There was another girl with her, a little shorter and a little browner, but her back was to me as we approached. From behind I could see she had the body of a dancer and her dark hair braided in cornrows.

Yvette had on a white-flowered sundress with a pair of matching platform sandals. It was the kind of dress that showed everything was in its proper place. If only I had met her first.

"Hey baby," she said as she reached up to hug E. He kissed her the same way he had in the foyer the night before to let everybody in the mall know that it was his.

"You go to lunch yet?" E asked.

"Why would I when you called and told me to wait for you?" She paused when she spotted me out of the corner of her eye. "Hey Thai," she said. "Welcome to my world."

I laughed. "It ain't that big of a world," I said. I imagined her Huxtable parents had made her get a job in the mall for the sake of being responsible.

"Tell me about it," she said. "Let me introduce you to somebody." She turned to the other girl, whose back was to me, and as if on cue she turned to me in slow motion. I knew who it was long before she turned around.

"Alicia, I want you to meet somebody." She smiled when she saw my face. But it was the kind of smile you give when you find something to be cute but not really funny. I felt a little tense, since I hadn't called her yet.

"We've already met. Haven't we, Thai?" She was mad that I hadn't called her but it had barely been a day.

"Yeah, we met at your party the other night," I said.

"Then I don't have to introduce you again," Yvette said. "But look, Alicia honey, can you be a dear and cover for me so I can go to lunch with *my* man?"

"Sure," she said quietly, as if she was about to mumble something under her breath after Yvette was out of sight. Her man? I gave E a knowing look and he kind of shrugged at me like there was nothing he could say. Charlotte had one of Shaw's finest going soft.

"And Thai can keep her company," E added with a smile, unaware that I'd already made a friend for the length of my vacation. I had been brought in as the diversion man for E's food court interlude. But I was also diverting myself from getting back to Robin. But I didn't mind. He was my boy and in Charlotte I had nothing but time to burn.

"All right," I said, giving him the nod. They disappeared down the mall toward the food court. I turned to Alicia.

"So you doin' any better? I mean after the thing," I asked.

"I guess. Ain't had to take an Advil all day."

"You told him yet?"

"Ask me that in a year and I'll probably still say no."

"You ain't gon' tell him you got rid of his baby?"

"It was a long way from bein' a baby. I ain't really even told myself yet."

"What you mean by that?" I asked.

"I still wanna be pregnant and I don't want that empty space inside me to be there. But I know it's for the best." dark

"If you say so."

"So I guess you don't know how to call nobody," she said.

"I figured if I called you the next day you would've thought that I was tryin' to hit it."

"And what would've been wrong with that?" she asked.

"You got a man and you just got rid of a baby. There's a little bit too much around you already for me to be thinking about that."

"Never heard a man say nothin' like that before," she said.

"I just know about gettin' cheated on and I don't want nobody to feel it the way I did."

"What happened?" she asked.

"Somethin' that shouldn't have," I said.

"You can tell me," she replied.

"I know I can," I said, "but I won't."

"You got somethin' to hide?" she asked.

"Yeah. But I think you do too. Anyway, you ain't tell me you worked with Yvette."

"You didn't ask. You didn't ask me much about anything the other night besides what I told you."

"Sometimes I just like to sit back and figure out stuff for myself," I said. "You gotta be like that sometimes where I'm from."

"Is DC that bad?"

"What you mean?"

"Is it like they say on the news? Do people be getting killed every night? When I hear about it on the news they make it seem like it's worse than New York."

"It ain't all bullets and bodies but it can be a trip. E could tell you that."

"That's where you know Enrique from? DC?"

"Since I was nine."

"Y'all don't seem like best friends."

"You ain't been around us enough."

"That's true," she said.

As we talked I made the city seem worse than it was. I turned every time I'd seen a gun into every time I saw somebody get shot and every time I saw somebody shot turned into every time somebody was shootin' at me and my boys. I wanted to impress her, and where I was from that was the way you impressed girls if you didn't have money. I was sure she didn't want to know that I was starting to like Charlotte's quiet nights and carefree days. I gave her what I knew she wanted to hear.

She looked at me more with pity than interest. Even though she was from New York she seemed sorry that my life was so "ugly."

"Your mama must pray for you every night," she said. She looked into my eyes for a something that wasn't there.

"Yeah," I said.

Other words were exchanged. We talked about what mall-goers were wearing and the heat and how she got her job. I didn't want to tell her about mine. With her I didn't have anything to hide. After all, she didn't even know my last name.

dark

E yelled as he slapped me hard on the shoulder. It startled me and I jumped. "You been standing in the same spot for a hour!"

"You didn't tell me he was so jumpy," Yvette commented. I gave her a look that said she could have kept her comments to herself.

"She's fun to talk to," I said. Alicia smiled.

"Well, you must be special, because she never says anything to me," Yvette said. I turned to Alicia and she gave me an affirmative look.

"So what's up for the weekend?" I asked.

"I gotta work, but what about Thursday? That's my next day off."

"Tomorrow?" I asked.

"Wednesday comes before Thursday, don't it?"

"You know, you ain't gotta be a smart-ass about everything," I said.

"Just call me and maybe I'll listen to all your complaints."

"I'll try," I said.

E finished up the goodbyes and we were on our way out of the mall. "Your mama must pray for you every night," Alicia had said. I always wondered if she did.

"So what's up wit' you and Alicia?" E asked as soon as we were outside the mall.

I shrugged. "Met her at Yvette's little thing the other night. She seem cool. She got a boyfriend, though."

"You know there was never a time when that woulda stopped me? Yvette had a man when I met her too."

"Well, I'm done wit' all that after what just happened. I had a broad cheat on me and it don't feel good at all. It made me kill a nigga, a nigga whose boys is probably in the street lookin' for me right now."

"Her cheatin' ain't make you kill him. Fuckin' around wit' Snowflake and Cuckoo made you kill him. Get it right. Who put the gun in your hand? And when you got a gun in your hand them niggas'll make you use it." Then he laughed.

"Man, this ain't no joke," I exploded. "This is serious, E."

"I know it is, but jokes is the best way I can deal wit' it. Every time it comes across my mind it scares me to death, and it ain't even my life."

"Yeah, I know you feel me. But I'm the one livin' it and I'm the one that can't hardly sleep at night without no nightmares."

I wanted to tell him about the dream, how I was at the other end of that .380 pistol. But I put the thought on hold as my building drew nearer through the windshield.

"So what you 'bout to do?" I asked.

"Business. Nothin' but business. Gotta go over to one of the buildings and talk to the super about something for Moms."

"All right then," I said as I jumped out of the jeep.

The heat from the sidewalk pushed through my New Balances, and hunger pangs ripped through me like a hooked blade. So I went down the street to the Burger King and got a combo meal. I ate there because I wanted to be around people, even if most of them were white. Then I came back and went into the building.

dark

87

As I reached the top of the stairwell I heard it faintly. The sound vibrated through the walls and bounced off my chest before it actually made it to my ears. It was a guitar, but not the loud hard rock kind or the country music kind. This guitar had some soul. I didn't know the song but it still got my attention. There was a note on the door to my apartment. It read: "I'm back—3F." I grinned and headed down the hall. The song grew louder as I approached. The amplifier had to be right in front of the wall, because the whole left side of the building shook along with each chord.

Despite the noise every door on the floor was closed. Sure it was the middle of the day, but I wondered how many people actually lived in the building. In three days I hadn't seen much of anyone, except for one dude who looked like he'd been on a two-year drinking binge who lived right across from Robin. He didn't look like much of a conversationalist anyway.

I stood in front of 3F devilishly thinking about what was waiting for me behind that guitar. This time I felt like I was twenty-five. That song was for me. I knew it was for me.

The door was cracked open and it backed away from the frame when I tapped it. I entered. The amp was right behind the door. She was sitting on the living room floor in those same sweatpants and nothing else, a glossy black guitar with gold trim in her lap. She stopped playing.

"So what are you here for this time?" she asked.

"I just wanted to know what song it was," I said.

" 'Walk on By,' " she said. "Isaac Hayes. You ain't never heard it before?"

"Nah."

"I hope that's not all you came for?" she said. I looked down at her nearly perfect breasts.

"You don't believe in bras?"

"Depends on the occasion."

"And what occasion is this?"

"It's the day before I don't have to go to work so I can let my breasts be free and have more fun than Wonderbras usually allow."

"I didn't know you could play the guitar," I said.

"You don't know me," she said with a grin, "so how would you?"

She was right. I didn't know her. I had known her even less the night before. I was probably just one of many men she used to feed her various hungers, a combo meal for the road. But what I wanted to do still felt right. I got down on the floor and took the guitar from her lap. Feedback exploded through the amp, so I snatched the plug out.

"Don't break the—" she started to say. I gently pulled her to me and ran my tongue across her lips until she invited it in. Then I tasted the wine from the empty glass that was sitting next to her. That taste alone made me stop thinking about my mama and Congress Heights and the new E and the old me and everything else that was pressing against my temple like a loaded gun.

"I almost gave up on you," she whispered.

We did it right there on the floor. She had two rubbers in those same sweatpants. I did it from the back again because I liked the way her hips moved when I went into her and when I came nothing mattered anymore, at least not for about twenty minutes. She wasn't a viable cure or a treatment option for my problems. But she did make them disappear for a while.

"What's the thing that scares you the most?" I asked in the afterglow.

"What do you mean by that?" she asked.

"Everybody has somethin' they're scared of, and since you seem like you ain't scared of nothin' I figured I'd ask you."

"I don't know who told you I was Supergirl. I get scared like everybody else."

She took a deep breath and plopped down on the arm of the cream sofa we'd just done it against. "Not bein' in control? That's what I'm scared of. You know, being in a situation where you have to depend on someone else, like the way my aunt was, but not necessarily just being sick. My mama didn't have any control over her life because she spent too much time trying to make my father happy. It wasn't until he left us both that she started to live her own life. That's what I'm scared of, having somebody take what's mine and me not being able to do anything about it."

"Is that why you came out here? To like try and be somewhere where you could be in control?"

"I came out here because my aunt who hooked me up

with the airline said that they needed people out this way. That's the only reason I moved. I'm not running from anything. Are you?"

"I'm just runnin' from goin' back to work next week," I said with a grin. But I had hesitated, and I got the feeling that she knew my real answer.

I got up and put on my boxers and my shorts. The air was as humid as usual as I rose to my feet. I walked over to the window while she turned on the stereo. Marvin Gaye oozed through the speakers, "Trouble Man." That wasn't the song I wanted to hear just then.

"When'd you learn how to play guitar?" I asked to change the subject.

"Started in the fifth grade. Only had one guitar in the whole school and it was all scratched up so nobody wanted it, except for me, that is."

"Sound like you was a nerd or somethin'."

"I was just different," she said as she walked over and stood next to me. "Didn't you ever want something that everybody else didn't have?"

"Yeah," I said.

"What?"

"To go to college."

"You could do that. Why didn't you?"

"A lot of reasons."

"Like what?" she asked. She gently ran her hand across my chest.

"I didn't want to leave home. I don't want to go nowhere

dark

else and forget where I'm from. I ain't trying to forget what me and all my niggas been through."

She giggled as I finished.

"I used to have a boyfriend like you," she said. "He was real smart and he had a head for business and I was trying to get him to go to school and he said some of the same things you just did. He messed around and got caught up in the wrong place at the wrong time. Some of his boys got in a shoot-out with the cops somewhere while he was sleeping in the backseat of the getaway car. They gave him three years just for bein' there. He's out now, but last time I saw him he wasn't the same."

That wasn't the way I wanted to go out. I'd seen too many cats getting put in squad cars and never coming back. But the possibility firmly existed that I would soon be one of them, as I was in Charlotte dodging a murder rap. I was having nightmares about taking a man's life over a girl I wasn't even in love with.

She was still topless when she got up and stood by the window, her nipples protruding. I thought about a Round 3, but I could tell she wasn't in the mood. The more I thought about what she had said the more tense I got. The more tense I got the more I realized that she might have been right. There was one Newport left in the box in my shorts and I took it out.

"I got somethin' better if you want it," she said. I nodded, and she reached behind one of the speakers and pulled out a sandwich bag with a little weed in it and then walked over to the other side of the room. She got a cigar from a box on the coffee table. I hadn't smoked a good Bob in months. The weed back in my room was garbage. She split the El Producto down the middle and rolled the blunt faster than a flash of lightning, faster than I'd ever seen it done.

In fifteen minutes the smoke hung in a cloud just above our heads. She didn't smoke with me, but I took tokes big enough for the both of us, spitting out thick white puffs like a dragon. After that, for the moment, I didn't feel like I was on that clock that had been ticking loudly ever since Congress Heights.

Had it been Snow or Cuckoo? Which one of them had put that gun in my hand? I didn't know. I hadn't wanted to do it. I had been so shaken up by what had happened at the mall that I had just wanted the whole beef to end in whatever way it had to. I was still angry. I was perfectly prepared to hit him with a chair or a bottle or break his nose or stomp him into red wine in the alleyway. But I wasn't a killer. Death wasn't supposed to be a part of the equation.

I spent the rest of the day with Robin. We watched two movies and some sitcoms and before we knew it it was almost eleven. Another day had come and gone. Robin was asleep on her bed, but for some reason I didn't want to lie down with her. I closed the door behind me and went downstairs to the front stoop.

The night was dead. No cars passed, and the warm wind dark brought no sounds beyond its own huff. I wanted to do something, but my idea tank was empty. I just sat on the stoop until I dozed off.

My mama was never there to tuck me in at night, and Pop was too tired. "Mama still ain't home?" Raj had asked Dee on the small screen in my borrowed apartment. The studio audience laughed like hyenas. Dee answered, "Nah, not yet."

thursday

"was she really worth it?"
the shadow asked me. The gun seemed a little further away
from my face this time but his frame was as pronounced as it
had been before. This time the background took on more of
a bluish tone, like a cloudy sky just before dawn.

"I don't know," I said. "I know I ain't love her."

"But you don't know what love is," he said. Then I
woke up.

dark

your green Tommy Hilfiger," I said to E as we sat on his bed playing NBA Live on his Sony PlayStation. His room was three times the size of the one he used to have at home, his closet was full of clothes, and there were six old school Blaxploitation posters on the walls. He had the ones for *Shaft, Foxy Brown, Truck Turner, Coffy, Black Caesar,* and *Cleopatra Jones.* He had liked those movies since the eighth grade when his dad brought them home with their first VCR. The tapes had been thrown in as a bonus.

"What you wanna borrow all my shirts for?" he asked just as I dunked on him with Kenny Anderson. I was playing with New Jersey and he had Toronto.

"Don't tell me you done got stingy. A year ago what was mine was yours."

"You know I'm just fuckin' witcha," he said as I stole the ball from him again. I was up by fifteen and there were three minutes left in the last quarter.

"So what you need my shirt for?" he asked.

"I'm goin' out wit' Alicia tonight."

"Alicia who?"

"The one Yvette work wit'. I told you I was gon' see what's up."

"You mean the one wit' the boyfriend who broke somebody's jaw at the barbecue last month for trying to get her number?"

"What?" I said.

"She ain't tell you she had a man?"

"Naw, she told me, but you ain't tell me nothin' about

him breakin' nobody's jaw. Why didn't you tell me that when you seen me talking to her at the mall yesterday?"

"I thought you were gonna try to fuck her, not go out wit' the broad so you could get caught. Charlotte ain't that big, you know."

"We ain't goin' out nowhere really. She said it's a place she wanna take me too."

"You bring a burner down here?" A burner was a gun.

"Yeah, Ray Ray gave me somethin'. Why?" I asked.

"I might keep it under the seat if I was you. You never know what might happen. Broads is shady," he said.

"Down here too?"

"Same rules apply wherever you go, even Charlotte."

"I guess. I see you ain't carryin' no heat."

"That's 'cuz I got me a rich girl. I bypassed that whole problem."

"Alicia ain't rich as Yvette?"

"Nah, she seem more like us from what I can tell. She just got out of high school and she down here on her own. I figure she just tryin' to make it whichever way she can."

"You doin' a little more than just makin' it these days," I said.

"You might be right, but my heart still run on forties and government cheese."

ms. mehdi gave e the day off, dark
so we went back and forth between PlayStation and BET. Our brains soaked up fast breaks, body blows, and music-

video hoes until we were dizzy. That was the way a vacation should be. It was a change I was more than welcome to. It had been a long time since I could just waste a day. Between working and unwinding from work there were never enough hours, and I usually just spent most of my free time with Ray Ray out in front of his building.

Ray could talk about anything for as long as you wanted. The only things he didn't like talking about were people who had died and a girl named Sharon who had his baby, then broke his heart by marrying this Mexican dude. She took his daughter and moved to Philadelphia. Now all Ray had was Brianna, his other daughter. Any other conversation was fair game.

Me and E met Ray up at the Banneker swimming pool the summer before we started sixth grade. He was in there by himself stealin' wallets out of the clothes bags in the locker room. Being the stupid fifth-graders we were, we blackmailed him for all of ten dollars, enough for us to get new G.I. Joe action figures from the People's Drug down the street. He told us we had his respect, and not long after that we started seeing him around the neighborhood, always scheming on something with somebody. By junior high the three of us were playing ball together. And once you start working as a team the friendship comes naturally.

Out of all of us I think Ray Ray knew the most about love. Every girl he had he was with her for at least six months, and he'd buy them things and take them out to dinner when he had the money. And as you might figure, all the girls loved him for it, even though after Sharon he secretly hated all of them.

"Love ain't shit," he said to me one night, after we'd come back from a barbecue in the 640 part of Northwest where he'd run into one of his old girls. "You can have it and it can make you feel good but when it go that shit hurts."

"So why you keep doin' it?" I asked him as I took a swig from the forty of Colt 45 we'd bought. The brew kept me warm in the cold night air.

"It's like smokin' rocks. Once you hit one you keep looking for that high you ain't never gonna get again."

"You talk like a old man," I said. It was right after I'd met Sierra and right before E left.

"I'm twenty-one, older than all y'all little niggas, so I feel old. As long as God let me keep gettin' older I'm all right."

"I hear that," I said. "I hear that."

"So what time you pickin' her up?" E asked, bringing me back to the present.

"I told her seven. She said she was goin' to the hairdresser this mornin', so I'm pickin' her up from the mall."

"She got braids. What she got to do to her hair?" he asked.

"Get it rebraided, I guess," I said.

"Girls and they hair," he said. "I don't care about they hair long as they bodies are tight."

"Speak for yourself. Girls be lookin' nice when they get their hair done."

dark

"As long as they don't look like Alfalfa I could care less," he said.

"Well, you can say what you want, but since I been here I ain't never seen Yvette walkin' 'round without her hair done."

"But that's on her. I don't make her do anything," he said.

"Whatever," I replied, laughing.

I rifled through his shirts until I found the green Hilfiger and slung it over my shoulder.

"I'm ready to roll," I said.

He walked me out like a guest when I was used to finding the door. My Maxima sparkled in the sunlight from its wash and wax that morning. I had even wandered into a barbershop near the car wash and gotten a cut.

The barber had chopped it all off when I only asked him to take off half. Now it was a low Even-Steven with a trimmed beard to match. I stepped out feeling like I was about to go to the Prom.

"Got a date with a young lady tonight?" the barber had asked me as he surveyed my wig. He saw he had a lot of work to do. But we both stopped to look at a pack of cuties strolling past the window.

"Somethin' like dat," I replied. I smelled the hair and the disinfectant and I thought about my barbershop back in the neighborhood where your eight dollars got you a cut and two hours of classic stories, none of which were ever true. Plus you got the latest in bootleg movies and the occasional tape of a fight off their pay-per-view descrambler.

"Your girlfriend?" the barber had asked me.

"Nah, just somebody I'm kickin' it wit'."

"Kickin' it?" He chuckled to himself. "Well, that's all

right." He said it in a way that turned his words into a song. "Just make sure you don't kick your feet from under you and fall down. Women are dangerous."

"What?" I asked, confused.

"How old are you? Sixteen, seventeen?"

"Nineteen," I said.

"Oh, that's even worse." He started whacking away with the clippers. "The more you feel like a man the less you really are," he said.

The shop was empty, and at first I thought that he was running his mouth just to pass the time. But he was trying to tell me something important.

"If you talkin' 'bout wearin' rubbers—"

"I'm talkin' 'bout bein' blind," he said. "So blind that it makes you mad and so mad that it eats away at you. I'm telling you this because you got this look on your face like you don't know. And whenever I see that look I gotta give you the speech."

"What speech, man? I ain't blind about how these broads is. That ain't my story," I said.

"Well then, what is your story?" He turned the clippers off to brush away the loose hair.

"Look, man, I came in here from down the street to get a cut. I ain't blind or deaf or nothin'."

"Hey, I ain't tryin' to be all up in yo' business, young brother, just want to give you something that might save you some trouble someday."

d·a·r·k

"I guess I better listen. I don't need no more trouble in my life."

"You just gotta know everything around you," he said. "You know how even if there ain't no light in your house you don't hardly bump into nothin'?"

"Yeah," I said.

"That's the same way you should keep your life. You gotta live your life knowin' how to get around in the light and the dark. Some of these girls out here will have you in the dark fo' sho'. You said you was goin' out kickin' it, and that mean you don't know the girl?"

"Nah," I said.

"Well, watch yourself. That's all I can tell you. It's easy to get in trouble."

"You don't even know," I told him.

"I probably know three times the half," he said.

The conversation shifted to whether or not Jordan was really going to retire. Whatever it was that once again had me tense loosened its grip. I hopped out of the chair looking like a new man in the mirror, but I felt the same on the inside. By the time I got to E's the barber's words had dissolved into the shadow from my dreams.

It was almost six when I got back to the building, and I was supposed to go get Alicia at seven. My Right Guard felt thin and I wasn't going out with a girl musty, so I hit the shower again. As the cool water cascaded down my face I had visions of Alicia's man trying to break my jaw over going out with her. I laughed at the thought. Anyone who wanted to fuck with me, a Shaw representative, was only making it harder on himself.

The shirt fit just right when I pulled it over my newly washed and oiled upper half. I had sixty dollars in my front pocket and a new rubber in my wallet. I brushed my hair until my scalp was sore and the waves were showing. Then I closed the door behind me.

"you're supposed to be late,"
she said to me as she clicked the last padlock on the jewelry cart. The mall was empty, our voices echoing in the deserted space. She wore a cotton white button-up shirt and a pair of khaki shorts with brown sandals. Her legs were lotioned shiny.

"I ain't never late," I said.

"All men are late. That's what makes y'all men. Maybe you early tonight, but sometime you gonna be late."

"Whatever you say. So where we goin'?" I asked.

"Why you asking me?" she replied.

" 'Cuz when I called you you said you had someplace to take me."

"Oh yeah," she said. "I guess I forgot that I was taking you there."

"Where is 'there'?"

"The river," she said. "I wanted to go down to the river and chill for a while."

"It's almost dark," I said. "I ain't tryin' to get bit by no snakes or nothin' like that, especially not in my Hilfiger shirt."

dark

"Aw look at you, soundin' like a little girl," she said in a babying voice.

"I-ight, just show me how to get there."

the sun was a dark orange

as it took its slow plunge below the horizon. The remaining light seemed to spread evenly across the sky like a watercolor. We drove for what seemed like an hour with nothing but trees on either side of the interstate. We passed the city limits and plunged into the rural terrain of the rest of Mecklenburg County. E told me that was the last stretch before redneck land. Then the river itself came out of nowhere.

"I told you it creeps up on you," she said, smiling. She seemed giddy about our destination.

"You ain't lyin'," I said.

I drove over the bridge to the other side of the river. That was in another county, but since the cops weren't chasing me it didn't make a difference. I took the next exit and drove through a series of twists and turns until we ended up in a parking lot next to the bridge we'd just crossed. From there we stumbled down a dirt path to the river itself.

It was the cleanest, quietest water I'd seen since I went on a field trip to Great Falls in the ninth grade.

"So what do you think?" she asked me as she perched herself on a dry log next to the shore.

"I ain't never seen a river this clean," I said. "You don't really want to get this close to the water at home."

"I'm from New York, remember? So I know what you talkin' about." She looked off into the darkening distance across the water.

"So how the hell did you end up here?"

"You won't believe me if I tell you."

"No, I'll probably believe you," I said.

"Probably?"

"If you start sayin' you an alien or somethin' I'ma have to take you back to the mall."

"Nah, nothing like that. I came down here because I wanted to grow up," she said. Her cornrows gleamed in the fading light. "I wanted to work and pay my bills for a while."

"How come you didn't go to college?" I asked.

"I just ain't ready. School was always boring to me. I especially don't feel like listening to teachers tell me stuff right now."

"You seem like you're smart enough to get in."

"I got in. I just didn't want to go. I woke up one day my senior year and I realized I wasn't doing what I wanted to do. I was doing what everybody expected me to do. I was messing with the kind of boys everybody wanted me to mess with. I wasn't supposed to be that kind of girl. So I started to wonder what would happen if I did what I wanted to do for once. I thought about it and I realized that I'd been on vacations and trips to a lot of places. But I'd never *lived* anywhere else, you know?"

"Yeah, I feel you," I replied.

"So I had cousins down here at UNCC going to school

and they wanted me to come down for a weekend," she continued. "I ended up staying a whole week. For me this is the kind of place where you can grow up and that's what I'm trying to do. I been here three months and I'm still workin' on it."

"Your parents just let you go just like that?"

"An accountant and a carpenter letting their daughter run off to a brand-new city at eighteen years old? Not my parents. I had saved up money and said I was just coming down for that visit and once I was down here I told them I wasn't coming back. I had a job and an apartment and I wasn't worried about eating, so how much could they really say?"

"My pops would've whipped my ass over the phone for doing something like that," I said. "But I guess I would've told him."

"You real close with your fatha?"

"He all I got," I said. "I never knew my mama."

"You didn't tell me that. How did that happen?"

"I don't want to talk about it."

"Why not?"

"I just don't want to."

"That's sad," she said, looking out at the water.

"That's just life. I mean, you down here livin' on your own. I know you done gotten knocked down a few times yourself."

"I done got knocked down but I fell out when I killed my baby."

"I thought you said it wasn't a baby yet."

"I change my mind from day to day."

"You wish you hadn't done it?" I sat down next to her when a lukewarm breeze brushed across us.

"I don't regret anything," she said, "but something grew inside of me and I ended its life. I'm a killer and I have to accept that."

"Everybody got things they ain't happy about, but you gotta move on."

"It ain't like getting over your last boyfriend." Her body tensed up. "I was gonna have a little boy or a girl. That isn't something you get over overnight."

"Why did you—"

" 'Cuz I didn't want to have *his* baby. The condom broke and—"

"If he's so bad then why you with him?" I asked.

"I'm eighteen. He's twenty-four and he has money. He takes care of me so I can save my money and get back in school."

"So you playin' him?"

"No, I care about him."

"Then you usin' him?"

"He's usin' me. He wants my ass and not my mind. Besides, he's too selfish to want to have a baby."

"He told you that?"

"I just know," she said.

she was selfish too. dark

That was the one thing I knew about her. She seemed like she wanted what she wanted when she wanted it. I was there

107

on that log because she wanted something from me. I knew that too. But despite her explanation I still couldn't figure out what she was doing with her man. Her words seemed unsure, like Qualie Madison's at that dinner table. I also thought about his breaking somebody's jaw at a barbecue. What would he have done if he'd found out she'd killed his baby? What would he do if he knew she had told the truth to a perfect stranger like me?

I sat there next to her in front of the moving water with the moon beginning to glow, and the moment was right for something special. But nothing happened. Instead I kept looking behind me to make sure the man in question wasn't hiding in the trees somewhere. After all, there was no one from the neighborhood standing there on the shore to save me if I got into something.

Her man's name was Diamelo and she had met him on her second day working at the mall. His lines were weak but he was brown-skinned and six-two and he hit the weights, so she let his weak game slide and gave him the number. They'd been together ever since because no one else had come along. By Christmas she'd thought she would have the money saved to make some kind of a change for herself. It didn't happen and she said she was stuck. After two hours sitting by the river I figured out that what she wanted from me was to squeeze her out of her situation.

"You know you can trust me, don't you?"

"Why, ain't nothin' to trust you for," I said.

"I mean if you got anything you want to talk about you

can tell me. What I got to lose? I'm a killer." It was like she was prodding me for a confession. Did she and Robin see the smoking gun tattooed on my sleeve or something?

"Stop all that killer shit. You can't go to jail for what you did."

"But I still killed."

She didn't know what a killer was. She had spread her legs and had someone do the killing. I pulled the trigger myself. That was the difference. I had a final face etched in my memory for life. She had a bunch of afterthoughts about what could have been. She wasn't a killer, and if she thought she was I wished that she would come to her senses.

"So you got a girl in DC?" she said in a massive change of subject.

"I broke up wit' her before I left."

"That why you came down to see Enrique?" she asked. "Got your heart broken?"

"You could say that."

"Did you love her?"

"Naw, I ain't never been in love," I said. I remembered my dream and I remembered my conversation with Qualie Madison. "I don't think I know what bein' in love is."

"You ain't missin' nothin'," she said. "It ain't nothin' but trouble."

"And I got enough trouble in my life," I said. "Besides, I don't think I'm the kinda nigga you fall in love wit'."

"Why?" she asked. Now I could only see the sliver of her

face lit by the moon. The rest of her was a talking shadow. We were both dissolving into the falling darkness.

"I ain't never bought girls no flowers or no candy or nothin'."

"Love ain't got nothin' to do with that. I just think you ain't never been that close to nobody."

I scratched my freshly cut scalp and watched her silhouette speak. There wasn't a sound down on that river except for the occasional whoosh of a passing car on the bridge above.

"It's gettin' dark down here," I said. When I pushed the light button on my Indiglo watch the hands said that it was almost nine.

"What's the matter? You afraid of the dark?" she asked.

"Nah," I said. "I just don't want to break my ankle goin' up that hill."

"I guess I can understand that," she said. "Let's go."

we scaled the hill like monkeys, moving left right left, trying to make the trip as quick and easy as possible. When we got back to the car, silence crept over us, and we remained in its grasp until the Charlotte skyline came into view.

"My dad wouldn't like it down here," she said. "Not enough tall buildings for him."

"That's probably why my dad would like it. He don't like tall buildings."

"Are you a lot like him?"

"I can't really tell. Maybe if I start workin' as a bartender or somethin' it might come out, but I'm me and he's him."

"I guess."

"Do you want to have another baby?" I asked her. The question caught her off guard.

"Where did that come from?" she asked.

"You said you had an abortion 'cuz you felt like you had to. Do you want another baby?"

"Someday, but no time soon. You want a baby?"

"I had one."

"Had?"

"It died way before he was supposed to be born. My girl had a miscarriage."

"I'm sorry," she said.

"You ain't have nothin' to do with it. But knowin' what I know now, it was for the best. No matter what happens it's always for the best in the long run."

"That's true," she said. When we got into the car she pushed the tape into the deck and OutKast blared from my muffled speakers. She ejected the tape.

"Not what I was looking for," she said.

"Then what is," I mumbled.

it was almost ten-thirty

when I dropped her off. She stayed with her man in an apartment on the south side of 77. He was still at work. They lived in a nice building. It had a security door and everything. It was even nicer than mine. I didn't go in or try to kiss her. But

dark

111

she smiled and gave me a hug and told me to call her. I told her I didn't have a phone. She told me that I could find a way. As I drove off I wondered if our babies had gone to heaven. Maybe God had figured that I wasn't ready for a son.

My temples throbbed by the time I headed back up the stairs to Apartment 3C. For some reason all I wanted was my bed. But as I approached the entrance to the second floor I heard this weird humming, like a song I knew but couldn't name. E didn't hum, and Robin wasn't the type to be humming in the hallway either. I approached with caution, but as I turned the corner something hit me straight in the face like a Metro train and everything went to black.

"Nigga, you betta stay the fuck away from my girl," he said softly. My vision returned moments later but I couldn't get up. What had he hit me with? I felt the blood streaming from my nose but when I touched it it didn't seem broken. I tried to get up but nothing would move. Then I passed out again.

"toni-i-i-i-i-i-i! toni-i-i-i-i-i-i-i-i!" a voice yelled, followed by the pounding of a fist on a door. I was lying in the same place but my joints were working again. My feet scrambled against the floor to get me to my feet. Blood was crusted on my upper lip, and something at the back of my neck hurt.

"Toni-i-i-i-i! Open the goddamn door before I kick it in!"

It was the man from the end of the hall, and he was banging on Apartment 3D like Toni was about to get evicted. I used the wall to help me get to my feet.

"Don't nobody live there," I said.

"Toni-i-i-i-i-i!" he yelled again and jabbed the door twice with his right fist. "Open the fucking door!"

"I said don't nobody live there, man!" I yelled. He stopped, turned, and took a few steps toward me. The smell of whiskey was in the air, the cheap kind Pop said rotted your insides.

"She always home," he mumbled before turning towards the door again. "She always home."

"Whatever," I said before I dragged myself to my doorframe and turned my key in the lock. He was still just standing there when I closed the door behind me.

As I washed my face in the bathroom I tried to remember who or what had hit me. I barely remembered where I parked my car or how I had gotten up the steps. But I did remember that anytime danger is waiting for you outside of your home, it meant that more of it was destined to follow. My nose wasn't broken but there was this numb feeling all the way through its upper half that for some reason made me feel nauseous.

I went downstairs and across the street to the pay phone. I checked my messages and found nothing, then decided to call Snow. But when I dialed his number it kept ringing. His mother never remembered to turn on the machine, even though Snow had bought it for her two years before. Then I called Ray but there was no answer. It had been four days and no one was around. I decided that in the morning I would take matters into my own hands. But when I got back upstairs I was tired. I lay down on the sofa to rest my eyes and the Sandman snatched me under.

friday

it was early, a little after nine, and once again I was nervous. My seat stuck to me as I sat in the periodicals section of the library. The broken air conditioning on the first floor made everything seem warm and stale. The moment of truth gnawed at my heels and the time had come to determine what my future would be.

The library copy of the *Washington Post* looked like it had been thrown eighty yards and spiked in an end zone. I flipped past articles on the upcoming Black Family Reunion, Bill

Clinton's latest exploits, and an editorial about pornography on the Internet before I got to the Metro section. It was Thursday's paper, and every Thursday the DCPD printed a listing of all the crimes committed during the previous week as well as details and descriptions of any suspects. I was reading the paper to see if I would find my name in those listings. Of course I prayed it wouldn't be there.

First I checked the stats for Northwest to see if anything significant had happened in the neighborhood. There had been an act of arson up on Meridian near the reservoir, two shootings in Petworth near Roosevelt High School, and three burglaries on three parallel streets off of New York Avenue. There was nothing about Shaw. I grinned. It made me smile that it had been one of those weeks when there wasn't any drama. But as my eyes shifted into Southeast, fear slapped my smile away and I took my gum out of my mouth and pressed it against the bottom of my chair.

Southeast almost always had the largest number of crimes, so it was the hardest to get through. Murder ran through its packed and dirty streets like water through pipes. Ray even used to joke that you got guns from the grocery store over there. In slow motion I ran my eyes over each and every one of the six homicides listed, and once again I imagined squad cars and sharpshooters at my house while they waited for me to blow back into town.

There had been a double murder by drive-by on Naylor Road, a stabbing in front of a liquor store on Good Hope Road, a wife clubbing her husband to death in Barry Farms, and then there it was, a shooting in an alley behind 2346 Blossom Street in Congress Heights.

Nicholas Washington, eighteen, had been found shot once in the head outside of a party. But there were no suspects. There were no suspects! I almost jumped out of my seat, but then guilt set in and my body instantly weighed an extra twenty pounds. A man was dead and I was still responsible. But for once I was glad that Snowflake had been right.

"Niggas ain't gonna say shit," he had said to me while I stuffed my clothes into my Dunbar High gym bag. He took a final pull from his cigarette and extinguished the butt in the ashtray by my nightstand. There was three hundred dollars in twenties on the bed that I'd saved for a rainy day, and there was the FedEx envelope E had sent me with the key to the apartment along with directions to it.

"It was too many people there to be sayin' that," I said. "I gotta disappear for a minute."

"If the cops do come looking for you and you done left, what you think they gon' think?" He had a point, but it was one I was already prepared for.

"I'm officially on vacation. I called and said I had an emergency with my family. As far as they know I got family in Charlotte. And if they ever ask I'll say E is like family to me."

"I guess, man, but if I was you I'd put my vacation on hold, find some pussy to get up in, and go to work like none of it ever happened. They ain't got no murder weapon and I know they ain't got no witnesses." dark

"How you know all that?" I asked.

" 'Cuz I threw the heat in the river and anybody who was up in the party know that if they open they mouth and I find out about it they won't be openin' it no more."

He meant it. He'd killed before. He'd even told me who he had killed, so I knew that doing it again was nothing. But still I didn't want to take any chances. Sure the gun was sleeping with the pollution-contaminated fish. Sure I had been a dark-skinned male in a dark room filled to the brim with dark people. But I had killed a man. I had shot a hole in his head, and that had brought me over to the Dark Side.

I don't remember a time when Snow wasn't on the Dark Side. I can't even tell you how or when we met him. He was just there one day. I think he made us his brethren because none of us had ever asked him for anything. We fought our own battles, and one time he said those were the only kind of people he wanted around him. He could do anything from stealing cars to slinging crack. And I'd seen him use all of his talents more than once.

But it appeared as if I had won the first round even though there was sure to be more to come. If it turned out that the cops weren't looking for me, I knew that whoever had hit me in the face the night before definitely was. And while my memory was about as organized as a bunch of papers in the wind, I had a feeling that it had to do with Alicia and the jawbreaker from the barbecue. I wanted to leave it alone by not going out with her again, by not even going to the mall again. She was cute but she wasn't worth the trouble. But now this shadow man had gotten the best of me, and

that was something I couldn't put up with. Nick had learned
that the hard way, and the Jawbreaker was asking to be next.

after two fixes,

Robin had me hooked. Sitting in the library at ten that
morning I wanted another hit. But Robin was flying the
friendly skies and would remain up there until nighttime at
least. Any thoughts about Alicia were associated with my
still-aching nose, so I didn't even think about calling. Lust
had to go on hold.

From the library on 5th Street I walked up Tryon towards downtown. I had planned to stop but my feet kept going. I passed a corner store and bought a honey bun and a
bottle of Snapple and called it breakfast.

I had never thought of downtown Charlotte beyond being a bunch of big buildings thrown together just so Charlotte could be called a city. But as I walked through it now
and really took it in I came to a conclusion: I wasn't at home.

LaShonda wasn't in front of the O Street market with her
little son Raquis and Mr. Jones and Mr. Mitchell weren't sitting in front of Ray Ray's building smoking their pipes and
talking about things that happened before anyone on the
block had been born. Instead of what I was used to all there
were were white people with funny southern accents who
bounced from one side of the street to the other painted in
navy blues, blacks, and grays as they mumbled to themselves   dark
about meetings and such. No heads turned as I passed. No
one yelled across the street to get my attention. No cops

stopped me to ask me if I'd seen somebody. No one knew who I was and they didn't care to know.

After six blocks the skyscrapers disappeared and I trudged past the *Charlotte Observer* building to get a look at the freeway from the view on Moorehead Street. I emptied my Snapple and tossed it into a gutter, where the bottle shattered. Then I turned and looked back the way I came. No one else was around. Snow and Ray Ray were miles away. So were Pop and Sierra and everyone else I knew. I didn't even feel like Thai Williams standing there, but like I was living someone else's life for a week. I had never traveled that far. No matter where I was in the city I always felt like I could turn around and see my house in the distance. I couldn't see a thing that was familiar, and it made me scared.

Back when I was ten, Pop didn't want me running the streets after dark. I always had to stop playing ball or stop playing Nintendo or stop talking to the other dudes on the playground whenever I heard those streetlights start to hum. E had to follow the same rule, so we left together even though our houses were in opposite directions.

Pop only made me come in because he wanted me to be safe. Even at ten I somehow respected that. But as I would make that walk up 7th Street towards the house I used to imagine that dark creatures were chasing me down the street. But I would always outrun them because I knew that I couldn't fight them on my own.

The thing I feared the most when I was ten was that one day I might wake and no one would be there for me except those dark creatures who chased me home at night. I felt that same fear a half block shy of Moorehead Street ten years later. As I stood there I felt like those demons were all I had left. They had chased me every night without laying a finger on me. I had beaten them home through fists, bullets, and broken hearts only for them to corner me on a strip of foreign soil. They had finally caught me, because I was on my way to becoming one of them and there was nothing that I could do about it. I turned around and started back towards my building. Damn Sierra. She must have been one of them.

"Was she worth it?" the dark shadow had asked me in my dream. I mouthed his words over and over again, hoping that they would take me back to Kansas or Shaw or a place where I didn't feel like my little world was coming apart. But instead they took me somewhere else altogether, back to where Sierra and I had started.

i was lost.

When I first started working for Public Works they had me going around with the sewer workers, and somehow someone had messed up the address to where we were headed to check some possible busted pipes. The official way to find the right spot had to do with using the numbers on the manhole covers on a map, but it was my first week and I just wanted to get the van to where it needed to be so we could get it over with. I came to a stoplight and there she was.

Sierra stood on the corner of 14th and Colorado with her girlfriend Stacy waiting for the bus. She was wearing a dark blue sundress with matching sandals and her hair was long but pinned up like a Japanese girl's might be. I asked her if she knew where 13th and Delafield was, and she told me. Then she showed me something else.

"Don't my mama pay taxes for you to know where you goin'?" she asked.

"If you ain't got nothin' nice to say you shouldn't say nothin' at all," I replied.

"I'ma say what I want to say," she said. I was leaning out of the window and I could already hear the other guys in the truck getting restless. They were all older and most of them were married and we had work to do.

I wanted her. But it wasn't just because she was cute. It was because I knew that I could get her. I had a job and I didn't seem like I was trying too hard and that was all I needed.

"Let me call you," I said without yelling it. I didn't have to use any lines or try to game her, because as far as I was concerned the digits belonged to me.

"What you wanna call me for?" she asked, grinning.

"So I can teach you some good manners," I said.

"I already got good manners," she said as she pretended to be looking down the street for the bus.

"I'll make them better," I replied. She smiled and walked over to the truck. I shook her hand and wrote her number down.

"I don't think you can teach me anything," she said.

"You can learn something from everybody," I said. She smiled and I drove off.

Regardless of what she said she had wanted to learn. She

122

didn't know exactly what I could teach her but I was eighteen going on nineteen and she was barely seventeen and somewhere in between there I had picked up some knowledge that she didn't have.

She lived in Northeast, off of Rhode Island Avenue near the main post office and the car impound lot. Her big brother was in the Navy and only came home for Christmas and Easter. Her parents worked for the government. She was in the communications program at McKinley and she wanted to go to college to be a newspaper reporter. She had two or three friends she was really close with and she worked as a shampooer at a hair salon a couple of days a week after school. That was all of her story. Her life could be summed up in a paragraph after all the hundreds of hours we'd spent on the phone and all the nights she'd spent at my house and all the kisses and the sex and plans about what the next level might be. And while it might have sounded like it was serious, in almost a year I never mentioned the word "love" once. Then the rubber broke.

She got pregnant on her birthday, which was four days before Christmas. We did it on the floor in my room because she thought that the bed made too much noise. And it was good. She was always tight and that gave me a chance to really feel it. But that night I felt it a little too much, because when I pulled it out the whole tip of the rubber was missing. The pregnancy test said "yes" and I was about to have a baby. While most dudes would have panicked I was happy.

I wanted it to be a boy. Every man wants a boy because he wants another him to be in the world. That boy was the only thing I talked about to everybody for those two months. But I never talked about her. I never thought about her either. I gave her everything she asked for and took her out and we talked about the future, but all I thought about was the seed in her womb, while she never talked about it at all.

Looking back, I think that she was scared, like I should have been. She was scared that she would never go to school or hang out with her girlfriends the way she used to. She was scared that I didn't love her, and most of all she was scared that because of me she was never going to be anything but somebody's mother. She had reasons to be scared, and I never did anything about them. Ray Ray had one child and another on the way, and Snowflake had too many, so it wasn't really a big deal to me.

But on the last day of February she woke up in the middle of the night bleeding and her stomach was on fire and when I got her to the Hospital Center the doctors told me that she'd lost the baby, even though they couldn't figure out exactly what had gone wrong. She didn't say a word to anyone for a week, and then she started to go on with the rest of her life. That was probably where the Nick thing started. Our baby was dead, and since that was all I ever talked about to her we had probably died with it.

Maybe Nick saw her on the street like I did or when she was shopping at the mall. Maybe one of her raunchy-assed friends set it up, thinking that I'd never find out. But that hadn't been what had bothered me about it. For me it was about the respect. If I wasn't doing it for her, then she should have just broke up with me. That way she wouldn't have had to creep around and fuck the light-skinned pretty boy on her living room floor. She would have even saved his life. She might have even saved mine.

"who you lookin' fo'?"

he asked me from the stoop in front of my building as I was on my way to the door. At first I didn't recognize him, and then when I did I couldn't believe that he was asking me questions when he had been much more concerned about Toni the night before.

He was wearing the same clothes, and even the same Yankees baseball cap, as the night before. The dark circles under his eyes looked like they'd been made with a thick Magic Marker.

"What you mean who am I lookin' for?" I asked as I stopped right in front of him. He was propped up against the building fiddling with a tiny black Ace comb he'd taken out of his shirt pocket. "You still lookin' for Toni?" I asked.

"I'm always lookin' for Toni," he said solemnly, "but I'll never find her where I'm lookin'."

"Man, I'm just lookin' for somethin' to do," I said. I took a seat on the opposite side of the stoop and lit a cigarette. I didn't want to smoke but I convinced myself that it was the right thing to do.

"Get a job. That'll give you somethin' to do," he said.

"Already got one of those. This is supposed to be my vacation."

"What you take your vacation here for?" he asked.

"It's the only place where I get my hotel for free."

"Oh, so you must be the mystery guest."

"Who?" I was confused.

"Ms. Mehdi's son called me last week and said you was gon' be heah."

"You the super?"

"Don't see nobody else takin' care o' dis buildin'."

"I mean I just thought you just lived here. That's all."

"Nah, I work here tryin' to live. But what you lookin' for, boy?" He took out his own pack of smokes. They were Lucky Strikes in the hard box, the same kind my granddad used to smoke. That, for some reason, made me want to hear more of what he had to say.

The scent of cheap whiskey still hung faintly but noticeably in the air around us. I wanted to ask who Toni really was, but I had a feeling he wasn't ready to tell me. I took a deep pull from my square and listened.

"Just lookin' for a place to relax," I said.

"What you need to relax for? What you got to worry about?"

"My father says life'll kill you if you don't relax," I said.

"So how you been spendin' your vacation in this *luxurious* city of ours?"

"I just came back from goin' for a walk."

"You must really ain't got nuthin' to do, huh?"

"Nah. I wanted to try and learn the city a little bit, so I went walkin' this mornin'."

"You learn somethin' while you was out walkin'?" he asked.

126

"Yeah. It's different down here, ain't like home."

"And where's home?"

"DC."

"Well, you right. Charlotte ain't as fast as DC. But I don't think you been here long enough to know how different and similar them two places are. Besides, you probably don't know nothin' about nothin'. I got drawers older than you."

He was probably right. Even though it was my entire life I knew that nineteen years was nothing in the scheme of things. Pop said it was less than the beginning.

"Well, can I ask you a question since you so old?"

"Ain't old people supposed to answer all the questions?"

"You got a lot of regrets about your life?"

"Everybody regrets somethin' or else you really didn't *live* life. You know?"

"I just did something I shouldn't have and been thinkin' about it."

"One thing? It'll be a million things before you my age. Didn't your mama tell you that ain't nobody perfect?"

I wanted to tell him that I didn't know my mama but I just nodded. He didn't need to know. Just like he didn't need to know about Nick.

"You right," I said confidently. "You right."

"You'll find it," he replied. "When you ain't lookin' for it you always find that peace you lookin' for."

"I really just want that peace, peace and a job I like and some girls who ain't tryin' to play me."

dark

"You ain't gonna find all that at the same time. And you don't get total peace in life till it's over."

127

"That's the way it seems," I said as I stood to my feet. I felt like I had had enough wisdom for the day.

He told me he was originally from Little Rock, Arkansas. He had been in the Marines and had fought in Vietnam. He had always been good at fixing things, so when a business venture fell through and he needed a job a friend of his led him to Ms. Mehdi, who made him the super for the Tryon Street property. He liked short thick women, and he loved Frankie Beverly and Maze, whom he had seen once at RFK Stadium during their first tour in '78. He had lucked up on a weekend pass for the show while he was stationed at Quantico.

Unlike Sierra I knew that there was a lot more to his life than what he told me and I wasn't going to learn it all from small-talking on the front stoop. That wasn't the way things worked with older dudes like him. So I pretended like I had something else to do so I could head upstairs without being rude. I slowly started twisting my body towards the doorway.

"One last thing," he said.

"What?"

"You gonna have some times when you get lost, young-blood. It's all right to get lost."

"What's your name, man?" I asked.

"Bill. Just Bill."

"All right, Bill, I'll holler at you," I said as I finally opened the front door and entered.

When I got up to the apartment I checked the Beretta again. As usual it was just the way I'd left it. I even checked the bullets in the clip, but they were the same too. As the days had passed I looked at it more as something I was holding for Ray than something I'd have to use. I studied the way it was made. It fit the human hand perfectly. All it took was one bullet to kill, and I had seventeen. I could kill seventeen people with a four-pound piece of machinery I could hold in my hand. That was a trip.

"This is my favorite shit," Ray had said, scratching his bald head as he watched me load the car. "I'm givin' it to you so you'll bring it back. You know?"

I didn't want another gun. But I wanted Ray to know that I had enough love for him to do what he asked. It was the nicest gun I'd seen. It wasn't scratched up or nothin'. Of course the serial number was filed off, but that went without saying. Snow and Ray Ray had both stood in front of my house and watched me drive off like parents watching their kids go off to school. I think deep down he felt bad about what had happened. He and Snowflake had never wanted to bring me over, so the best thing he could do was try to keep me out of danger, which meant keeping everything quiet and making sure that all mouths were shut. They were my true niggas and along with E I couldn't have had better friends.

Bill had said that there were some times when you got lost, and I tried to think about what he meant. I had found my way down Tryon and back. I had found my way to Charlotte without any major problems, but what I hadn't found were all of the reasons why. Why had it come to my joining the Dark Side and holing up in an efficiency in Charlotte, North Carolina? "It's all right to get lost," he had said. It was all right to be lost.

if I really want to do this," I said to Robin after we were more than ten blocks away from the building.

"You said you wanted to get out the house," she replied. "I'm gettin' you out the house."

This night "out of the house" meant more white people at a party for Delta employees. Two baggage handlers were hosting a BYOB night of beer and board games, and none of it sat well with me. I imagined everyone at the party looking and talking like Qualie Madison. The thought made me strongly consider going back to sleep, which was what I had been doing ever since I came in from my little stroll on Tryon. But stupid conversation and white-people music were my only way out of 3C. I would have rather watched reruns of *Gilligan's Island*. But Robin had asked me to come. That made the trip worth it.

"You don't like trying new things, do you?" she asked with one hand on the wheel and the other fumbling with the stereo. "Love TKO" from Teddy Pendergrass came out from somewhere.

She had on a snug white T-shirt with a bottle of Tanqueray on the front, a pair of baggy jean shorts, and a Polo cap with the brim pulled down over her eyes. Short tresses of her sandalwood hair poked out from the sides of her hat.

"Not unless I have to," I said.

"You need to be more open to things. You might not be so lonely if you were."

130

"I ain't never say I was lonely."

"You don't have to," she said.

She rocketed down 77 like a bullet in her hunter-green Eclipse. By the way she drove you'd have thought there was a bomb at the party only she could disarm.

"You don't have to," she repeated. "I can read it off that cute little face of yours."

"Anything else you can read there?" I asked as I lit my first cigarette in six hours. She wanted a drag before it was barely between my lips. I gave her what she wanted. After all, she had me hooked.

"Yeah, I been thinkin' about it. I think you only down here 'cuz you felt like you had to. I don't know what you up to but I know you think you gotta be here, at least for now." She took another drag and then passed it back to me.

"What you think I'm hidin'?"

"That's your business," she said. "Long as it ain't got to do wit' me I ain't got no questions to ask. I learned how to keep my mouth shut a long time ago."

I still didn't know her. I'd slept with her twice and I didn't know her last name. But she had said the right things at the right times and she knew how to shut up and let me deal with my own problems too. That was hard to come by in a girl where I was from. It made me a little sad to think that when I left I'd be leaving her.

"Why you ain't got no man?"

" 'Cuz if I get one I gotta keep him and keepin' men is too much work when you trying to do what you want to do," she said.

"What it take to keep a man besides not trippin'?"

"It ain't never that simple," she said. "The way I look at it if you talkin' 'bout men and women there ain't never no short answers."

"Y'all women always be makin' love more of a big deal than it is," I said.

"How would you know? You told me you ain't never even been in love. Plus you don't know nothin' about women."

"As far as love go you right. I don't be takin' it seriously. If it happen it happen. If it don't I'm better off."

"You think you know everything but it don't seem like you know much at all." She chuckled to herself. "So what, you don't never wanna get married?"

"Why should I? My pops didn't and he turned out all right."

She shook her head. "What? You think your pops didn't get married because he didn't want to? Settlin' down with somebody is some difficult shit to do. There's a lot of things you have to consider."

"Like what? It ain't that hard," I said. "You love a girl enough to wanna get married and then you get married. If it work it work. But most times it don't work."

"The reason it don't work is because everybody runs around thinkin' that it's just about love when it ain't. You can be in love wit' somebody who get on your nerves. But it's about bein' able to get through problems with that person. If you can't get through problems then it ain't worth nothin'."

"You been married before or somethin'?"

132

"Nah, but I know too many people who have."

"They all still together?" I asked.

"Most of 'em got divorced."

"See, that's why I ain't pressed to do it."

She couldn't help but smile. What I had said made sense and she had to admit to it.

"You still don't know nothin' 'bout women," she said.

We came off of 77 and went past a mall and a movie theater before we got to a group of adobe condos jammed on a narrow street across from a firehouse. My behind ached from sitting too long and I was glad to get out of her car.

"So what's the deal with this joint again?" I asked her.

"Brad and his roommate Tim are two of the baggage handlers who work for the airline. They're just havin' a little somethin'. Me and Brad started workin' around the same time, so he invited me. Believe me, I'm just here to load up on the free drinks."

"But you said it was BYOB."

"Yeah, everybody else is bringin' it, and they know better than to try to charge."

"You be drinkin' and drivin'?" I asked.

"Yeah, but I know how to handle mine, so I'll be all right," she said, grinning. I respected her confidence.

We walked through the open complex gate past a small fountain and up a flight of stairs. The place seemed harder to get to than the Batcave and my patience was thin. I didn't want to be around any more ghosts, but I did want to be around Robin. So like I said before, it worked out. dark

"And I thought you were going to stand us up," Brad said

133

loudly as he opened the door. His goatee barely connected and his dirty-blond hair was tied back in a ponytail. He was wearing a short-sleeve button-down with a pair of khaki shorts and beckoned us in like a butler.

The smell of beer hovered in the air-conditioned air. I didn't say a word to Brad. Instead I just gave him a nod and a grin and walked in behind Robin.

"This your boyfriend?" he asked her before we were barely into the foyer.

"No. He just lives in my building," she said. I frowned at the way she had put it.

It was a small gathering. Five men and women were piled on top of each other in a game of Twister in the middle of the living room. Three of them were white but there were two token blacks at the bottom of the mat. One had her hair dyed green even though she was dark-skinned. I didn't speak to her at any point in the night.

Robin said a few hellos and passed through the living room dwellers. I followed. I could see that a few people were outside on the small metal deck. But the majority were in the kitchen crowded around a tall pale-faced white boy who reminded me of John Stockton except he had a receding hairline.

"And the guy says, 'Are you gonna bang her or watch me drool?'" The crowd of ghosts exploded into laughter. We had walked up too late to get the full joke. An Asian girl with un-usually light brown eyes pulled Robin to the side as I moved closer to the kitchen commotion. Tim looked like John Stockton but he had a voice like Shaggy from Scooby Doo.

"Hey, you want a brew?" Brad asked from somewhere behind my left ear. I nodded.

A long-haired blonde and a short-haired redhead flanked Shaggy Stockton on the right and left, their arms glued to his waist. When there were no more jokes the crowd fanned out towards the Twister game but the girls stood their ground. There was a sweating-cold Heineken in my hand when I paid attention to my left palm. It appeared the same way the .380 had. I took a swig and marveled at the taste of quality beer. It was a long way from Mad Dog and St. Ides.

"What you starin' at?" Tim asked in my direction before exploding into laughter. I could tell he'd had a few too many. Had I been at home his words might have been grounds to start something. But I was alone in a room of white strangers. That made me think twice about any potential boxing matches.

"Nothin', man, just drinking my beer." I turned and went out on the deck.

"So how about you give me those seven digits," a silhouette with a goofy voice proposed to another female outline in the darkness on the deck.

"I don't think so," she replied. "Even when you're drunk your jokes aren't funny."

I giggled to myself. With his ego crushed he moped past me and walked back into the living room.

"Don't y'all ever learn?" the faceless woman asked me as she took a swig from her bottle.

"I can't talk for nobody but myself," I said.

"I can actually respect that," she replied. "But I swear to God, the first guy who comes up to me with something original is the one who I'll get married to."

"Is it that serious?" I asked. She laughed to herself.

"I don't know," she said. "It might be."

"So you work wit' Brad and Tim too?"

"No, I'm a flight attendant," she replied. I still hadn't seen her face and I didn't want to see it. She was just another apparition.

"So you know Robin?" I asked.

"Yeah, we fly together all the time. You her boyfriend or something?"

"Nah." I paused. "We just live in the same buildin', so she invited me to come with her."

"I've been over there a few times but I've never seen you when I was there."

"I just moved in. I just wanted to get out of the house tonight."

"You should try my job, then you'll never be in the house long enough."

By my fourth day in town I had gotten good at small talk. The words came from someplace that had been left unused at the house with Pop and at work and in front of Ray Ray's building. With the people in my life almost everything went unsaid. If you were there to say "What's up?" that meant you were doing all right, and if you weren't getting evicted and all the utilities were on it meant you were really all right. You always wanted to be more than all right but you could settle for survival.

With us we talked about things that had happened. Who was messing with who? Who got shot? Who got arrested? Who had moved in or moved away? Where was the party for the weekend? We didn't need or want anything small to talk about for the sake of being polite.

But in this new place there were words and questions and uncertainties. There was a homie-lover-friend with a hunter-green Eclipse who had dedicated her life to herself. There was a best friend from my side of the river who was swimming in a brand-new ocean. There was a man who banged on doors searching for a mystery woman called Toni who told me that it was all right to get lost. All of them had something to say, and although I thought all my words had been drowned out by that one shot that split Nick's wig open, when among strangers I had to act like I had plenty to say, just for the sake of conversation.

I traded words with the faceless silhouette as she finished her bottle. Then I finished mine and we stood there making stupid comments about the heat and life and the hangover Shaggy Stockton would have in the morning. But small talk did have its advantages. Somewhere between figuring out if either of us had ever won a game of Twister and how many flights she'd flown I came to a simple conclusion that seemed complex: The world was a big place.

The white woman without a face didn't have a clue as to how I lived. I didn't have a clue as to how she lived either. The rules of black and white didn't change from state to state. Neither did the game of life. Shaw was a speck of sand on a long beach made up of nothing but space.

Her faceless form faded into the whiteness of the living room and I was alone again. Robin had said that I spent too much time alone. That had bothered me. She didn't know about Snowflake or Ray Ray or E and how a day didn't go by when I wasn't with at least one of them. She also didn't know that it had been because of the fact that I hadn't been alone that Nick had died. If I had been by myself the gun would have never entered my hand. If I had been alone I wouldn't have been at Freddy's "rest in peace" party in the first place. But the one thing she did know was that I was hiding and she knew that when you don't want to be found the only thing you have to look at is yourself. So just like those nights when I had to be in before the streetlights went on, I was finally on my own. Every move I made was a crucial one.

"What you doin' hidin' out here?" Robin asked softly into my ear as I stood still against the deck railing. I could tell that she had a little something in her system. Her words sounded slightly slower as I stared at the outline of the moonlit trees behind the condo.

"Just lookin' at the sky," I said. "It's a nice night."

"You bored already?" she asked.

"Nah, just thinkin'."

"About what?"

"Life is short and you never know if it's gonna end quicker than you thought."

"Yeah? And?"

"Well, what would you do if you got up tomorrow and

you was in a whole different place with all different people and you didn't know what to do about it?"

"I'd do whatever it took to get wherever I wanted to be." She pressed her body up against mine. "It might take me a little while to figure it all out, but I'd get it done. I couldn't sit there and just cry about it."

She dug her chin into my neck. I thought about the aunt she had come to Charlotte to take care of. I imagined her confined to a bedroom and having to send Robin to get everything for her. Robin became her arms and legs and fingers and feet. She in part became the woman herself to help her get through. But still she had died and now Robin kept everything at a distance because she had been too close. Even at nineteen I could read that. She had chosen the cop-out way of dealing with losing somebody. But I was a killer. So who was I to judge her?

"Hey you two lovebirds, we're about to play some spades," Tim shouted obnoxiously from the other side of the sliding screen door.

Robin gave him a look like he was asking to get a tap in the groin and then spoke. "Yeah, we'll run some with you, Tim. We 'bout to show y'all how it's done."

I didn't know that white boys even knew about spades. To me it was the blackest game you could play, and Brad and Shaggy Stockton were trying their hand just to get whipped. I'd throw the deck out the window before I'd let some white boys beat me.

"Are we nit-picking or just playin' straight up?" I asked.

"Straight up, dude. This ain't for money or nothin'," Brad replied.

"All right, let's do this," I replied.

I dealt first and managed to give Brad and Shaggy the best hands of their lives while Robin and I barely scraped together four books. The cycle repeated itself for another three hands and the score was minus fifty to two hundred.

"Why the long faces, chumps?" Shaggy said to us. He must have thought he knew me well enough to talk trash without pissing me off. But he didn't know me well enough for those kinds of jokes. After his little remark every book they won brought me daydreams of me making him eat the cards. But in reality they were eating me.

When we hit minus fifty I looked at the score and felt helpless. No matter how well Robin and I put it down we were still destined to lose. But there was too much at stake to take a loss.

That was how I had felt when I walked into Sierra's on that night. When I saw them there on the floor I discovered that I could never do enough to make her happy. It would have happened even if I had loved her. I didn't want to lose. I didn't mind losing her but it was the idea that another man had beaten me that drove me crazy. Nick had crept up from behind while I was getting a second wind and lapped me. It had been Snowflake's idea, but I wanted to go up to the Gap and show him that while he might have been faster, I was stronger. I wanted to beat that message into his bones as they cracked. I wanted to press it into his jaw, maybe even have a tooth of his around my neck as a souvenir. I wanted to make Nick understand that he could never beat me. I was never going to lose, especially not to him.

"How many you got?" Robin asked me. Tim had dealt me both jokers, the deuce of diamonds, and six spades. I didn't have any clubs either.

"I can get you six," I said. "What about you?"

"Three," she replied.

"Let's run a ten."

"We'll go board," Brad mumbled.

God had dealt us redemption. Every card we dropped was the right one. They only ended up getting two of their four, and four hands later we put them out of their misery.

"Told you we was gonna show you how it was done," Robin said joyfully as we stood up after she dropped the small joker to bring it home.

"We had your asses in a sling there for a while."

"A while ain't good enough when you playin' in the pros," I said. Robin gave me five. Our next two hands sealed their defeat.

"Now, gentlemen, I think it's time we take our leave of you."

"You lucky bastards," Tim said.

"Luck ain't got nothin' to do with it," I said. "That's what you get tryin' to play a black-people game. Only way you gonna get us is if you wanna play some bridge or pinochle or somethin'."

They had to laugh, even if they didn't want to. They

knew it was true. Robin told me later on that Brad had learned to play at the mostly black high school he went to in Florida. She also told me that he'd tried to talk to some of the other black girls at the airline. That made me like him a little more. But Shaggy Stockton was still just a loser.

Half an hour later Robin and I said our goodbyes and headed back to our building.

"You were getting a little heated for a while," Robin said to me on the way back. "I thought you was about to hit Tim in the face."

"I don't like to lose."

"I can tell. But like my mama told me, winnin' ain't always everything."

"You right. But you gotta admit it feel good."

"Only when you get somethin' out of it," she said. "Winnin' just to win don't get you nowhere. Least I don't think it does."

"Yeah," I said.

It was barely midnight when we got back to the building. Robin had to fly in the morning, so she didn't invite me in. But she kissed me on the way to her door. I stood in the doorway and watched to make sure she got in all right and then I closed the door behind me.

In the dark I walked over to the kitchen and got the last can of Sprite from the fridge and opened it. I sipped it on the sofa and listened to the bubbling sound the liquid made inside of the open can. White boys could play spades. There was a whole world I hadn't seen, and winning wasn't everything. When the last cool drop of lemon-lime refreshment slid down my throat I lay back on the sofa and touched the spot where my face was still bruised. I thought about whoever it was who had hit me the night before and a bunch of questions surfaced that I didn't want to deal with. I told myself I'd find the answers tomorrow and drifted off.

saturday

"so when did
all of this happen?" E asked as he applied the second coat of
wax to his jeep. It was a little after two and he was giving the
4Runner its weekly beauty treatment.

"You be askin' too many questions," I said. "Somebody
stole me in the face and you talkin' 'bout when it happened? You should be talkin' 'bout where I can find this
nigga."

"Hold up," he interrupted. He draped his rag over the
driver's side mirror and turned to me.

"You down here worried about goin' up for murder one and you ready to start somethin' else? You ain't Ray Ray. You ain't Snowflake and you definitely ain't Cuckoo. What you need to do is leave that broad alone and go about your business."

I wanted to argue but I didn't have a leg to stand on. I had no way of knowing that it had been Alicia's man, but that seemed like the only logical explanation. Something needed to be done and the clock was ticking.

"You right," I mumbled to myself. "But if it was him, how did he know where I was stayin' at? It ain't like I'm in the yellow pages. Matter of fact I ain't even got a phone."

"Well, if we see him again we know what we gotta do," he replied with a seriousness I hadn't expected.

"I thought you wanted me to leave it alone."

"Don't go lookin' for nothin', but if it come looking for you you can't run from it. Same as it always was."

The last sentence was more for my benefit than for his. He knew that he had it easier now, and he knew that there was a little part of me looking for a way to prove that he wasn't as down with the neighborhood as he used to be. He said it to let me know he was, even though I knew in my heart that he hadn't changed that much.

"We ain't got to worry about all that just yet," I said as I took a bite from my double quarter pounder. "So what's up for the night? I'm tryin' to be around some black people. I was at this white party last night."

"How you end up at a white party?"

"This girl in my building took me over there. It was all

right. I had me a Heineken. Ain't never had no Heineken before."

He started buffing again, tracing over every inch of wax. I coveted his ride each time I looked over at mine at the end of the driveway. All the wax in Pep Boys and a gallon of Armor All couldn't bring my Maxima into the '90s. The paint on the roof had started to peel and the once chrome bumpers and hubcaps had become a dull gray. I should have been thankful. Snowflake and I were the only people my age on the block who had cars. But as I looked at that periwinkle paint with the V-6 under the hood everything I had seemed small. Back in the neighborhood E had to ask me for rides.

"You act like Heineken is Dom Pérignon or somethin'," he said.

"I just ain't never had it before," I said.

"You hittin' it?" he asked abruptly.

"What you talkin 'bout?"

"Come on man. This me. You know you didn't go to no white party with no broad unless you hittin' it."

"Now I got game. But you think I'ma be fuckin' girls when I only been here four days?"

"All it takes is the right girl. I don't know why you tryin' to act like I ain't known you since elementary school."

"All right," I said, throwing my hands in the air, "I hit it. Actually I hit it a couple of times."

"For real?" E asked with pride in his voice.

"Yeah," I replied, grinning.

I had come a long way in three years and E knew it. I had started off with a big girl named Stacy Andrews on the roof of Ray Ray's building on my sixteenth birthday. She was drunk and she said she wanted to give me something so I'd remember being sixteen for the rest of my life. It was awkward and sloppy but she did what she set out to do. I never forgot it and E was the only one I told.

"You said she stays in the building? She fine?"

"Man, she past fine. She'll make Yvette wanna sit down somewhere and get a makeover."

"I don't know about all that," he said.

"You ain't gotta know. You just gotta believe me."

"So what you gonna do?"

"I don't know, man. But I ain't gonna be here long enough to make her my girl or nothin'. Besides, she one of them broads that like to do what she like to do. She might not want to be bothered wit' me next week."

"You know what I say," he said. "Just hit it for as long as you can."

"I'm way ahead of you," I said. "I'm way ahead of you."

That night Dru Hill was performing at the Coliseum, Charlotte's big concert arena, and E was taking Yvette to the show. But afterwards they were going to a club and he wanted me to come along. I was told Alicia might also be coming. I told him to count me in. I didn't really like clubs but Robin was working and I didn't want to sit in the dark while the rest of black Charlotte was dancing the night away.

"You think he woulda hit me in the face?" I asked him, still preoccupied with who threw the infamous punch.

"Probably so," he said. His jeep was now fully waxed and he was sitting next to me drinking Kool-Aid from the pitcher. "If he one of those jealous boyfriend kind of dudes you know he's gotta run and tell his girl what he did."

"I think I should go ask her. Yvette workin' today?"

"You just askin' to start some shit, ain't you? You gon' go to the mall to get into it wit' Alicia and get my girl fired while you're there."

" 'Licia know how to be cool," I said. "She don't wanna get fired no more than Yvette do. Besides, if it *was* him she'd be as ready to fight as I am. She don't like him that much."

"That's what she tell you. Damn, ain't you learn that you never go by what a girl say?"

"I just need to know if *he* was the one," I said.

"Look, I ain't your pops. If you feel like you gotta go over there then you know I'ma go with you. But you're drivin'."

I needed to go. I didn't feel safe about going anywhere in Charlotte for the rest of my stay unless I knew whether or not I had an enemy out there waiting to catch me when I least expected.

I drove, charged by the Huck-A-Bucks tape that thumped through my rickety car speakers. E looked out the window for the entire ride, his face painted with concern. He was expecting the worst while I just wanted a simple an-swer to a simple question. If Diamelo claimed responsibility for tagging me, then I would know to cut Alicia loose and keep my eyes wide open in the streets for the two or three days I had left.

Like any mall on a Friday, Eastland's walkways were packed with scurrying shoppers and dawdling loiterers. It reminded me of the lower levels of Union Station on the weekends. Friday through Sunday, kids between the ages of twelve and sixteen window-shopped until they dropped, fed their faces in the food court, and developed new and different techniques to cut in the lines at the movie theater on the bottom floor. Crews would walk around in groups of twenty, none of them with more than train fare in their pockets. That never stopped them from going into every store that offered a glimmer of interest.

In the summer the middle-school girls with halter tops and jelly sandals walked around pointing and giggling at boys they liked. The twenty-plus crews looked for empty walls to look hard leaning against. It was the same throughout the mall, painted black, Mexican, and even a little white. The same scene replayed itself five hundred miles to the south.

With my mind at Union Station I temporarily forgot why I was there. The electric current of a teenager with too much time on his hands sizzled through me, and I wanted to turn the clock back to the point where it was as simple at malls and movie theaters as it used to be.

But my business was to find out what Alicia knew, and E's business was to make our trip to the cart appear to be nothing but social. He dragged behind me like a kid with a cavity on the way to the dentist.

"Just do this shit real quiet. All right?" he implored as the cart came into view. Alicia had on a Snoopy T-shirt and a pair of khaki shorts, while Yvette wore jeans and a baby T-shirt that showed her navel. Neither of them saw us coming.

dark

I walked past Yvette unnoticed. Alicia had just rung up a customer, and she noticed me just as she was closing the register.

"Hey," she said, smiling. "Ain't expect to see you up here today."

"Well, you never know where I might pop up," I replied.

"I see," she said. "You still ain't called me, though."

"I still ain't got no phone. But I'm easy to find. Lately it seem like people know how to find me all the time."

"Not me. I don't even know where you live."

"Oh yeah, I forgot about that."

She looked me right in the eye and her arms were completely still. I hadn't hit the nerve I was looking for yet. If she was playing stupid she did the best job in my nineteen years in the game. I was still cautious but immediately I started to look for another explanation for my Thursday-night knuckle sandwich.

"So I heard you're going to the club with us tonight," she said.

"Where you hear that from?" I asked, remembering that E had just asked me if I wanted to go.

"You forget who I work with," she replied.

"Ain't you a little young to be goin' to the club?" I asked.

"Young? Negro, all you got on me is a year and a fake ID."

"That's still an advantage," I said.

E looked in my direction every few seconds, hoping that his worst fears weren't about to bear fruit. I gave him an inconspicuous nod and his whole body relaxed. He turned back to Yvette for the duration of our chat.

"So what your man think about you goin' to the club?"

"I don't know," she replied, shrugging her shoulders. "Maybe I'll ask him when I come back. I don't really tell him about much of anything."

"Then why you got a man in the first place?"

"Like I told you the other night. I need a free ride. Men come in handy when you need that."

"So you usin' me too?"

"I'm not sure yet. But I'll let you know when I've made up my mind." She was joking.

She also didn't know what I thought she knew, but she was still dangerous. She cared less than Robin did, and that was an accomplishment. Furthermore when I combined the fact that her man had broken a jaw over a phone number with her general disregard for that same man's feelings it would have been best to keep my distance. But she was going to the club with us and I'd be damned if I was going to stay in the house like a punk.

"Well, I guess I'll holler at you tonight," I said with a dizzy feeling in the middle of my skull. I took one step backwards and felt like I might fall over.

"I'll be sure to wear something just for you," she said.

"You do that."

I spun past E and Yvette and began my trudge toward the car without a word to anyone. I'd dug up ten feet of sand but the treasure chest I'd come to the mall for had turned up empty. But the new mystery was yet to be solved. I had already killed one person. There was a brand spanking new

dark

151

Beretta under my sofa and now I was hanging around with a girl who had killed her baby and all her cares and concerns along with it. I really didn't need the drama.

E traipsed out to the car ten minutes behind me. His face looked twenty pounds lighter and he had a swing in his step. He was just glad his imagination was the only thing that had torn up the mall.

"So what she say?" he asked on the way back to his place.

"She ain't seem like she knew nothin' about it. I don't think she do."

"Girls can be good at lyin'," he said as he once again stared out the passenger window.

"I don't think she lyin' but I still think she's trouble. She's the kind that got a boyfriend who be gettin' all possessive about her even though she ain't thinkin' 'bout him."

"Girls like that get niggas shot," he said, shaking his head. "Remember the barbecue when I told you he broke somebody's jaw?"

"Exactly. And I ain't tryin' to be dead. Yvette goin' wit' us to the club tonight, right?"

"Yeah."

"I hope she keeps her girl in check," I replied.

"Either way you know I got your back."

"I hope that's enough," I said.

the sun was still high
in the sky at 5:00 P.M. and I was back at the library for the first time since checking the crime report in the *Post*.

I walked in and picked up the first book I saw and read it until I got tired. It was about money and how if you took a little out of your paycheck every time you got paid you'd always have something tucked away for the future. Then once you had a nice amount of money you could use it to make more money by investing it. I didn't understand some of the words and terms but the book took my mind off things and made me look toward the future.

I was already nervous about the night ahead. Every twenty minutes or so I thought about heading back to Apartment 3C to put the Beretta back in my waistband the way it had been Monday night. My left hand kept repeating the motion of pulling an imaginary trigger.

I hadn't had one of those dreams in two nights. I also hadn't thought of Pop since I'd left. What would I say to him without lying? If I told him the truth, all he could do was worry and tell me to come home. He might have even told me to turn myself in, and that wasn't happening. What kind of a helping hand could Pop lend me against a potential murder rap, two fine girls, and a phantom assailant who gave me the Mike Tyson in the third-floor hallway? I had to get myself out of this one.

After a while I closed the book and walked over to the magazine rack. The *US News* listing of the top hundred colleges caught my eye, so I picked it up and went back over to the table. As I read I didn't know most of the names except for Harvard and Princeton and USC and some of the state schools. It cost twenty or thirty thousand dollars a year to go to some of those schools. That was how much I'd made in a year at Public Works. From what I remembered UDC was less than a thousand dollars a year. I wondered what the difference was.

Either way I needed to get in school, even if it was just taking the classes to get my real estate license. Doing time in the filing department at Public Works was killing me slowly. E had been right. After a year there were three days a week I had to debate whether or not I was going to call in sick. Sitting in that hot office pulling, replacing, and reaarranging files took something out of me I wasn't sure I could get back.

Every day my supervisor, Jerry, shuffled back and forth through the office like an overseer in a cotton field. He was only twenty-seven but if you looked at him he could have been thirty-seven: bags under his eyes, gray hair, and a tendency to complain about things that weren't important. I had to do whatever it took not to end up like him. College was the answer.

Higher education had been E's and my secret dream. A classmate of ours named Kendrick went on a college tour our tenth-grade year and he came back like an explorer telling of a new world.

The black college life was it. He told us about the girls and the classes and how all the students spoke to each other in passing instead of just the people from their blocks or families. After that we wanted it more than he did. He never made it either. He got his girl pregnant the April before graduation and ended up working for the post office to take care of his kid.

But we didn't want the black college life bad enough to

leave DC. That narrowed our options to Howard or UDC. Howard was too much money, and we didn't think we had a chance at scholarships. So we chose UDC. January 1, 1997, we had the catalogs and applications and everything. But E left and I never filled mine out.

Other things got in the way. It was around the time that Fat Tony got shot near the reservoir behind Howard while he was trying to buy some weed. The dude who shot him put the word out that Tony had pulled a gun on him first. In a week there was a beef between all of Shaw and all of 640, the neighborhood where the marijuana salesman resided. After that the cops caught Ray Ray standing out in front of his building with a .45 in his hand. They tried to give him six months. The judge let him walk with probation and community service because it was his first offense. The DC jail overcrowding problem didn't hurt him either. Snowflake's girl had another baby and it wasn't his, so for three weekends straight we went out looking for the baby's father. To make a long story short, college went on hold. We had to do our thing for the neighborhood.

I photocopied a few pages from the magazine and stuffed them in my back pocket right before the library closed. When I looked at my watch I couldn't believe it. I was far behind schedule.

"Ain't think I'd see you again this soon," Bill said. He stood in the lobby wearing a dingy T-shirt and overalls with a huge toolbox in his hand and a Discman around his neck.

"Somebody makin' you do some work today?"

"Think I got dressed up like this to go to church? Little white girl up on the fourth floor got a short in her light switch."

"You mean Qualie?"

"You know her?" he asked.

"Yeah, she the first girl I met in this buildin'."

"You ain't fuckin' her, is you?"

I laughed. "Nah, man. I don't do the white girl thing."

"Just gotta make sure nowadays. I think my son got him a white girl. Won't never show me no pictures of her, so either she ugly or she white." He paused. "Niggas'll jump in bed with anybody that's breathin'."

I was glad to see him. I felt like I could talk to him and it didn't feel awkward. I felt like he knew me, and very few people made me feel like they knew me.

"So when you gettin' outta here back to . . ."

"DC," I said.

"Yeah, DC. When you goin' back?"

"Probably in the next couple days," I said while I fiddled with my keys. "I ain't sure yet."

"Need to make up your mind before your free room and board run out. You make a decision a lot faster when you gotta pay rent."

"I know that much," I said. "I just got some loose ends to tie up."

"What you? Sixteen? Seventeen?"

"Nineteen."

"What loose ends you got besides your shoelaces? I got loose ends I had to file bankruptcy to take care of."

"Problems is problems. I'm just tryin' to take care of what I can."

"You can't solve nothin' overnight. Shit, I still got problems. Some things you just carry with you the whole time you walkin' the earth."

"Like what?" I asked.

"Like Toni," he said plainly.

"Yeah, why was you yellin' for her the other night?"

" 'Cuz she still supposed to be there," he said solemnly.

"What you mean?"

He looked off over my shoulder at the street outside. "Some things you keep to yourself. I'll be talkin' to you," he said.

He turned and started down the first-floor corridor past me and the stairs, even though he had told me he was going to the fourth floor.

"You ain't crazy, is you?" I asked as he walked away.

"Hell nah, I ain't crazy," he replied as he continued down the corridor. "You just don't know me yet." I shook my head and started up the stairwell.

It was approaching seven when I studied the Beretta on the coffee table again. My only Polo shirt was already draped over the back of the sofa and my only pair of Boss jeans were on the bed. I was ready four hours before I needed to be.

Somehow the weapon itself made me restless. I didn't want to be in the same room with it but when I was away from it it hovered in the back of my mind. I looked over at the door and aimed an imaginary gun at the peephole and pulled the imaginary trigger. Time was running out.

d a r k

I wasn't ready to go back to DC but I had to. In Charlotte there was more time than grass in a meadow. There were fine women who gave up the tail and there was a homeboy who had made something of himself. But there was also the hard reality of Congress Heights and the echo from a shot fired in an alley hundreds of miles away.

I took the gun downstairs and put it in the back of the car next to the spare. It was only a precaution in case anything went awry during the course of the night. Then I came back upstairs and dozed off in the humid air. I fantasized that Robin and I were doing things in an airplane bathroom, things you had to unfasten your seatbelt for.

I woke up just before nine but it was still too early. This was one of the first Saturday nights I hadn't spent sitting in Ray Ray's mama's living room waiting for him to get ready. For him taking a shower and putting on some clothes was a two-hour process. Since he didn't own anything but T-shirts and sweatshirts it made even less sense. After E left, Fridays were our night to let loose.

We'd go to clubs like Blossom's and Quigley's to try and meet girls from other parts of the city. Other nights we'd find a party or a barbecue if it was the summer. And then if there was nothing else we could always get some forty-ounces from the store and watch *Menace II Society* and *Friday* until three in the morning.

I hadn't talked to Ray since he had handed me the piece Monday morning. I hadn't talked to anyone despite several attempts. Pop was worried to death by now. I thought about calling but I knew he was at work until eleven and when he got home he'd off the ringer so he could sleep. I was his son. I knew better than anybody. But all the talks we had and the lessons he'd taught me I still didn't understand him.

Pop could have had everything he wanted. His dream of selling real estate was within his grasp but he never reached for it. Almost every single mother in the neighborhood wanted a piece of him from my first day at kindergarten on, but his dates were few and far between. He only had two friends, Thomas, whom he had been friends with since the seventh grade, and Leroy, another bartender he had worked with at Mel Krupin's, one of the places he bartendered when I was in junior high. No matter how hard he had to struggle he always seemed larger than life to me, like a hero out of a comic book who just happened to snore and have an obsession with T-Bone sandwiches from the Florida Avenue Grill a couple of blocks up 7th Street.

But while he was my hero, he was a simple man who might not have believed all dreams had a chance to come true. He had his house, a '90 Honda Accord he got at an auction, and the proud distinction that he was black and 100 percent debt-free. He was my pops, the only family I needed.

I hadn't called because I couldn't tell him the truth. To him Congress Heights was ample evidence that I hadn't taken any of his lessons to heart. I had given in to everything white people wanted me to by killing one of my own brothers. And I had to do it all without him.

Suddenly, I thought I heard Robin's footsteps in the dark hallway. But when I ran and opened the door there wasn't a soul in sight. She had flown from Charlotte to Atlanta to

LA, and was spending the night and then coming back on Sunday. There would at least be twelve hours before my next fix.

As I touched the still-sore areas of my face I again contemplated who my attacker had been. In no time I had directed all the evidence to Diamelo the boyfriend. I didn't know what he looked like but when I saw him he was going to remember my face.

"That nigga Ray Ray called me today," E exclaimed as he walked through the open door. By then I was dressed and ready. Since he had entered alone I knew that the girls were downstairs in the jeep. It was a good thing she was already seated in E's ride. That meant I'd have a nice Alicia-free ride all the way to the club in my own car.

"What? What did he call you about? What'd he say?"

"He was lookin' for *you*, said you need to talk to him soon as you can. But you know Ray Ray, probably just wanna tell you about some broad."

E was wrong about that one and I knew it. Ray never called out of state unless it was serious. Ray wasn't really even the kind to use the phone. He'd just come by your house or he'd see you when he saw you. Since the days when he sold crack he didn't trust the phone. On the phone anyone could be listening to you, especially with the miracle invention of three-way. And since I'd been trying to get ahold of Snow for days it all added up.

"You can call him on my phone when we get back. Man, hurry up. The girls is in the car," he said.

"You know I could have met y'all there."

"We *could* be there now too," he replied. "Plus we should take one car. Parking ain't no joke up there."

I forgot that the gun was in my trunk. I forgot the importance of having an Alicia-free ride. I also forgot my cigarettes.

Yvette sat in the shotgun seat with a slinky long black dress with a split up one side. Alicia was in the back with black stretch pants and a white silk blouse. Her eyes lit up like I was the tooth fairy when she saw me.

"How you doin'?" she asked, smiling.

"I'm all right," I said. "You been to this club before?"

"Yeah, I been a few times. It's all right but it can't mess with nothin' back at home."

"I don't think Charlotte can hang wit' New York when it comes to clubs," I said.

"You damn right it don't," she said.

"Why do you have to curse so much?" Yvette asked from the front. As much as E cursed I didn't see how it could bother her but I got the idea that she and Alicia were more coworkers than anything else.

The jeep went into motion and Toni Braxton jumped out of the speakers.

"What you mean why I curse so much?" Alicia replied.

"She from New York. What you expect?" E added.

"Fuck you, Enrique. All right?"

I laughed. I hadn't heard a girl say that to E since the ninth grade when he never got haircuts and used to bite his nails all the time. That was one thing I did like about Alicia. She didn't fawn over E like most of the other girls in Charlotte I had met.

dark

161

Silence fell over all of us for the fifteen-minute ride between my building and the club. The 4Runner rode so smoothly that we could have been on an airplane. I mouthed the words to "You're Makin Me High" as it played.

The Sugar Shack was tucked into a shopping center on Independence Boulevard. It had a storefront entrance with a long line in front. Very few were dressed to impress, so it looked more like a bunch of people standing outside of somebody's house party than a club. Too many dudes and not enough girls, the classic house party problem.

All of a sudden Alicia gripped my arm tightly. I wanted to ask her what the hell she was doing but I figured it wasn't worth the effort. I scanned the faces that scanned me as we moved toward the entrance.

I brought up the front and E had the rear.

"Damn, you in a rush or somethin'?" E asked. "I'm the one that's gettin' us in."

"From the looks of these niggas it don't seem like you gotta be *somebody* to get up in here. I ain't impressed with this joint at all."

"It ain't home but it's somethin'," he said. He brushed past me and went up to the bouncer. He said a few magic words and we slid in ahead of the thickening line.

Alicia's grip didn't weaken on the other side of the doorway. Something about her touch filled me with a panic I couldn't describe. It reminded me of what I'd felt that night in Congress Heights. I pulled my arm away from her.

"What's wrong with you?" she asked.

"Just wanted my arm back. You grip too hard."

Those were the last words I said to her before the boom from the speakers blasted away any dialogue the two of us might have had. I wanted to get away from her anyway. I felt like she was going to get me killed. Alicia, Yvette, and E broke off in one direction and I wandered in another.

The club was shaped like a shoe box with very little else to distinguish it from any other four walls with a DJ. The bar was on one side of the room and the rest of it was open space with a few colored lights hanging from the ceiling to give it the disco effect.

I found a cozy spot between the bar and the wall. Hardly anyone was drinking because the bartender was carding. But there was more than enough marijuana in the air to make up for it. The dude sitting next to me sucked on a blunt thicker than a broomstick.

"Want some smoke?" he mouthed with a thick backwoods southern drawl.

I shook my head and signaled the bartender. He bought my fake ID and brought me a cold Heineken for four dollars. The first swig went down like ice water. With the second my nerves unwound like a loose ball of yarn.

"This joint is getting packed," I said to Mr. Marijuana standing next to me. He nodded and then began the incredibly long process of coming up with an answer. The smoke had his train of thought moving at five miles an hour.

"Every Saturday," he said as he looked around the club.

dark

"It be like this every Saturday. And all the bitches ain't even got here yet."

"They better hurry up before they can't get in the door," I said.

"Niggas always make room for the bitches," he added and then exploded into laughter, putting his arm around me.

"You right about that, nigga," I said, "you right about that." He took his arm away and I lifted my beer again. The panic was gone and I felt good.

My eyes scanned the club for any traces of danger, but there weren't any I could see. I felt dumb for turning down my new friend's offer to smoke. Sure, it was against the rules to puff with a stranger, but rules were meant to be broken. After all, where I was from it wasn't every day that you came across someone who was willing to share their weed.

"Can I still get some of that?" I asked. He didn't say a word but handed me the blunt. I took a deep pull and the smoke dribbled from my nostrils and hung on the front of my face like a storm cloud. It was better weed than what Robin had given me. It might even have been better than what Snowflake used to get for us before the cops raided the neighborhood weed factory. It was good to be a little high, again.

Alicia seemed to come through the floor when she grabbed my hand and pulled me onto the dance floor, although I wasn't ready to move yet. But the lights, the Biggie Smalls song, Alicia's hand on my arm again, and the combined smell of perfume, deodorant, beer, and weed somehow heightened all my senses at once, and I fell perfectly into the rhythm of the song and moved my body accordingly.

Alicia giggled like a kid in a sandbox as our bodies complemented each other. I looked into her face and thought about Sierra and how she and I used to dance at parties the whole night without stopping. Then I thought about Robin and how our rhythm was perfect. It wrapped itself around us during each and every session and only unraveled when the afterglow spread across our bodies. I imagined Robin standing right in front of me, where Alicia was, her grown-up grin in the place of the Kool-Aid smile before me. I wanted to be inside of her right then, right on the dance floor. Alicia would just have to move out of the way.

Alicia turned around and started grinding her booty against me. I moved with it and put my hands on her hips and pressed her against me and held her there. That was when the fist smashed into the back of my head and made me see purple spots.

It took me too long to react. I knew that whatever I did I had to keep that fist from hitting me again. I spun around and fired a round of punches that smacked against the air and nothing else. An arm wrapped itself around my frame and pulled me back through the crowd. My arms flailed above my head as the crowd parted. I wondered where E was. But I knew that if something went down I had that Beretta right in my car in the trunk outside to handle things. That was all I needed.

My body smacked against the hot concrete outside. Pain shot through me but I got to my feet. I hoped that E had seen me. The line for the club was to my right and it was three times longer than it had been when we went in. But I should have focused on what was right in front of me as two jabs freight-trained into my face. I fell backward into the bouncer, who caught me and stood me back up. By then my guard was raised and I wasn't about to get hit again.

He was right in front of me. In the split second I took to examine his face I knew that he was a complete stranger and yet he seemed familiar. Either way I pushed off and hit him at least five times with everything I had. He stumbled backward but caught his balance and came back with a hook I didn't see until it was too late. I tried to block but his fist knocked my forearm away and smacked me dead on the jaw. I splattered into the asphalt like Jell-O. It was the first knockdown of my career in a one-on-one fight.

I had three seconds before he would start stomping me, and from the size of him stomping meant that I was going home on a stretcher. All I had to do was get to that trunk at the other end of the parking lot. I put everything I had into my legs and Michael Johnsoned my way down the parking lot. I knew he would follow. I intuitively knew that there were others with him. I wanted them to follow too. I was going to show them all that Shaw niggas weren't to be fucked with. I just had to get to that gun.

Being buzzed and partially high had not helped this high-pressure situation. I'd edited out the part of the night's events where I decided not to drive, leaving the pistol in my own car, far away back on Tryon. That was not a good thing to realize when I reached the end of the lot and I saw E's jeep parked instead of my Maxima. It was time for Plan B. Keep running.

I pushed myself down the lot's remaining stretch like my life depended on it. I juked past three cars across Independence Boulevard and burrowed through a bunch of trees into a set of woods. I didn't hear anything behind me but I kept running. I didn't want to take the chance that they were still there. My lungs wheezed but adrenaline carried me all the way out of the woods to a sidewalk, where I fell face-first onto the grass next to the curb.

I snatched oxygen in gulps, my eyelids fluttering as if I was about to black out. Where the hell had E been? By running had I left him to be a sitting duck? My jaw stung so intensely it felt like it was vibrating. My nose was bleeding too but it wasn't broken. I was pretty sure I had pulled a hamstring while I was running. At the moment I wasn't in any shape to go up against the Terminator back there without a weapon that would end the fight quickly. Slowly but surely I got up.

I was in a borough of townhouses without a clue of which way to hobble to get back to Apartment 3C. I thought of knocking on a door to ask to use the phone, but it was after midnight. I was black and the chances were that someone would call the cops on me on general principle.

I headed west, walking around the woods I had come out of. I had never run from a fight before, but I had never stuck around to be in one I didn't need to be in either. Pop had taught me that. He'd also taught me to always have enough money in your pocket for a cab. I had the money but when I got back to Independence there wasn't a cab in sight. I took my Polo off and wrapped it around my waist to camouflage myself as best as I could. The Terminator was looking for a bruised and bleeding dark-skinned kid in a cream Polo, not a gray Toronto Raptors T-shirt.

I started down Independence away from the club and back towards Apartment 3C. Six blocks later I stopped at a pay phone.

"Who the fuck is this!" Ray Ray yelled into the phone just as I pulled it away from my ear.

"What's your ass so mad about?" I asked calmly. I could feel the blood crusting on my upper lip. I remembered the feeling from the night before.

"Oh, damn, nigga, I ain't know it was you. Why it take you so long to call me back?"

"Don't even get me started," I said. "So what's up? Where the hell y'all been all week?"

He paused at the question. "Cuckoo and Snow got popped on Monday."

It took a second for me to get the meaning of the words. I had expected to hear that the cops were looking for me after all, or that someone had ID'd Cuckoo at the scene, anything but them getting shot instead of me.

"What? It was Nick's boys, wasn't it?"

"Nah, don't be stupid. They wouldn't think about comin' up here even if they knew how to find it. Snow and Cuckoo got shot when they was comin' out the carry-out up by Howard. Somebody just lit 'em up. Ain't have nothin' to do with you."

"They dead?"

"What's wrong wit' you, Thai? You know Snow can't

168

die. Bullet broke his arm, though. Doctor said it went right through the bone. If that shit had shattered he would have needed a new bone or somethin'. Cuckoo got it the worst. He took three in the chest and one in the leg. But he had a vest on, though. They say he's gonna be all right. All anybody know was that it was a blue Maxima wagon. Cuckoo got out the hospital yesterday but he went home like the doctor told him. Snow been out every night since Tuesday, walkin' around looking for that Maxima wagon on foot, with his shootin' arm still in a sling. I called 'cuz I was worried about you. I knew you was checking your messages but I just wanted to see if you was all right."

I knew why Ray wasn't out with Snowflake.

He explained that he was in the house taking care of Brianna. See, there were three things Ray cared about in the world: his daughter, his mama, and us. In that order. He had also called because he knew that the minute I got back home Snow would be ready to get us all together to tear the Northwest apart trying to find the dudes who shot him. He'd definitely pull me in, and since he and Cuckoo had covered for me with the Nick thing I'd have to go with him. Ray's call was a warning. But I wasn't exactly sure of what it warned against.

Ray Ray had been in the same building for his whole life. He could tell all the people who had lived on his hall in his twenty-something years of life, and he could tell it to you in detail. His dad had died of lung cancer when we were little dark and his mama was a secretary at a law firm downtown. She worked overtime so much that the only time we saw her was on the weekends, and that was if she wasn't playing cards with her sister who lived two floors down. They had a bunch of relatives that lived in their building.

Ray never thought about leaving, because everything he needed was right there. It was perfectly fine in his mind for Brianna to grow into adolescence looking at the same three rooms he had. No one had told him any different, and I wasn't one to tell people what they should do. He stuck to Snowflake because Snow wouldn't leave either. Snow had more influence on the playground that was in the middle of our neighborhood than he would ever have in any other place in the whole world. That was why they tried to keep E and me out of what they did. But they knew we couldn't stay out forever.

But Snow *would* find that blue Maxima, eventually. It was one of the things he was good at. But it wasn't my thing, and Ray Ray knew it. He wanted me to stay put for a few more days before I came back, long enough for Snow to find his man or give up trying for the time being.

"Yeah, I know," I said. "Seem like trouble follow me wherever I go."

"You ain't have to use my little friend yet, have you?" He meant the Beretta.

"Nah, not yet, but I don't know. Got mixed up with this one broad down here who got a boyfriend, and you know how that go. I just got into a scrap with him and he this big nigga that make Cuckoo look little."

"Damn nigga! You got your ass whipped?" he said, giggling.

"I hit him a couple times, then he got me once and I ran. His boys was wit' him too."

"Well, when you put it that way I wouldn't have stayed around that long if I ain't have no gun on me either."

"I had left it in my trunk back at my house."

"Hey man, you talked to your pops?" he asked, changing the subject.

"Nah. Left a message Monday night but I ain't hollered at him."

"He worried." He said it in a way that told me that Pop was really nervous. "He be calling me every night asking if I heard from you."

"Well shit man, I just be feelin' like I'ma have to end up tellin' him about what happened. Knowin' Pop, he's gonna want me to turn myself in."

"Then I hope you ain't tellin' him shit."

"Hell nah."

"So what's up with E? He all right? I only talked to him for a second."

Ray Ray and E were the least close out of all of us. There wasn't any personal beef between them. Ray knew E through me. I brought E into the crew and he and Ray Ray were two dudes who wouldn't have hung out if they hadn't known me. But at the same time he almost had as much love for E as I did. We all felt it when he left.

"He more than all right," I said. "He got a 4Runner and all dis gear and he got a girl that's twenty-two and he make twelve a hour, plus he's about to go to college down here." dark

"He livin' like that? I might have to make me a little trip down there myself. He's livin' phat like that?"

"You gotta remember his mom's got a real estate company."

"I'm just wanna go down and see all this for myself."

"I hear you. But for real man, how you been? You workin'?"

"Yeah, I ain't tell you before I left. You know I took the postal exam?"

"Nah, when you do that?"

"About three weeks ago. I start up at the main office on Brentwood next week. I'ma be sortin' mail in the back, but the money's good."

"That's good, man. Hope I got a job to come back to."

"Just call in on Monday, say you missed your plane or bus or somethin' and come back on Tuesday night."

"But you said I shouldn't come back."

"Just don't tell Flake you here for a while."

"I guess. But look man, I gotta roll. I'll holler at you."

"All right," he said.

Brianna was crying in the background as I hung up, and I remembered when she had still been inside Ayanna's stomach two years before. Time flew. Ray had found out she was pregnant on the Fourth of July the year before when we were all down at Haines Point watching the fireworks at the monument on the other side of the park. She had grown and he had changed as she grew. He was more responsible and a little less crazy. Snowflake was the only one who was really hopeless. Even he knew it.

After I hung up I stood there and stared at the phone receiver as it hung in its cradle. Several cars whizzed by as they shot toward the Charlotte skyline. Even with a crew I was alone. Neither Snow, Ray, nor E could help me as I sat there contemplating the possibilities for the future. E had been right when he said that us watching each other's backs wasn't always enough. As a man you had to stand alone first. I guess it was then and there that I became a man. And men had to take care of their responsibilities.

I picked up the phone again. The next call was going to be a little more difficult. My hands trembled slightly as I dialed my calling card code and then the number. The pain in my bruised jaw heightened as it touched the receiver. He must not have hit me hard enough to break it.

I was ready to hang up on the third ring even though I knew he never answered until the fourth. It was almost one-thirty and even if he had closed at the restaurant he would have been in the house by now. The fourth ring was cut short.

"Pop?"

"And where in the hell have you been?" he asked.

Silence hung on my tongue before I answered.

"My fault, Pop."

"Damn right it's your fault. Out of the blue you go driving down to goddamn North Carolina and don't call nobody? You left here lookin' like you had done killed somebody in the first place and you even leave a number on the answerin' machine where I can get in touch with you?"

"Pop, you don't even know."

"I don't know what? That I been running 'round here asking Ray Ray where my own son at? What else don't I know? You ain't in jail, are you?"

Usually Pop was cooler than a fan. But when it came to me he could hit his boiling point in a matter of minutes. He'd had five days to get heated up.

I stood there sidetracked as I tried to figure out how I was getting home without bumping back into the Terminator and his boys and Pop wanted to tell me about what he was worrying about.

"I called you on Monday and left a message."

"Yeah, but how was I gonna call you back? You know Snowflake got shot?"

"Yeah, Ray Ray just told me. He's all right, though. So is that other boy that come up sometimes. The crazy one."

"Yeah, Cuckoo."

"I told you what was gonna happen to that boy. Told him too. But like I always tell you he gotta live his life his own way."

"You right," I replied.

His anger had slowly dissolved into his words and the tightness in his voice had relaxed.

"E is doin' all right," I said in an attempt to make everything feel normal.

"What you expect? His mama's in the real estate business. Now you see why I'm tryin' to get my license?"

"You gotta take the classes first," I said.

"I ain't worried about the classes."

" 'Cuz you don't never take the time."

"I'ma go. Soon as—"

"Soon as what? Soon as you ain't gotta support me? I got a job. If you need to cut down your hours I can pick up the slack—"

"We'll talk about that later. I just wanted to make sure you all right. You all right, ain't you?"

I could have told him the truth. I could have said that I was a killer and having killed was killing me. I could have told him I'd met a girl I liked and that I'd just finished running two football fields to get away from a jealous boyfriend with a first-rate right hook. I could have told him that I'd realized that there was a whole world outside of DC and Shaw.

"Yeah, I'm all right," I said.

"That's good. You comin' back tomorrow, right?"

"More like Monday. I got some things I gotta do."

"But ain't you supposed to go back in Monday?"

"I'ma call in. Got some things to take care of with E before I get out of here."

"You got loose ends after four days? You must be havin' some trip. Just don't get fired runnin' the streets with E."

"I won't."

"Well." He paused. "You nineteen, you gettin' to be a man now. You gotta take care of your own responsibilities."

"Pop?"

"What?"

It walked into my mind through a door I didn't remember opening. It climbed its way through my lungs and up my throat until I spit it into the receiver.

"You ever killed somebody, Pop?"

"Killed a lot of people in 'Nam. Ain't have no choice. It was a war."

"You shot 'em?"

"Shot 'em. Had to stab one once. Came out of nowhere, had to stab him with a bayonet. That's hard when you stab a man, because you feel that knife go in and you know that you did it and you gotta live with that for the rest of your life. You can shoot somebody from a mile away and not know what you're hittin'. What's all this killin' stuff about?"

I had to aim close without hitting the bull's-eye. So I tried something that hadn't worked in nineteen years.

"Me and E was talkin' about our mamas. And I was saying that I didn't know about my mama, if she died."

"You don't wanna know how your mama died," he said. My mother was dead.

"I wouldn't have brought it up if I didn't want to know."

There was something in my voice that neither of us had ever heard, something that had hurdled over the father-and-son safe zone. He didn't want to answer the question, but I think he knew the solution wasn't another trip to the liquor store.

"You think I killed your mama?"

"Nah, Pop."

"Well, I did kill your mama."

I flushed the words back out of my ears. I wound time back for a few seconds and started again.

1 7 6

"You heard me right, boy. And I'ma tell you what you want to know.

"I wasn't always a bartender, you know. When I got back from the war I started out workin' as a bouncer at this club call the Penthouse up on Georgia Avenue. It was a little hole-in-the-wall strip club all the Howard boys went to to get their little dicks hard. I was in a little better shape back then and I had come out the military not that long before so they gave me pretty good money to make sure nobody touched the dancers or got too rowdy. Delilah, your mama, well, she hated that job. It was bad enough that you were three months old and we weren't married, but I was workin' a job where she thought I was lookin' at naked girls all night, not knowin' that most of those girls weren't much to look at anyway.

"So one night this mothafucka walks in actin' like he owns the place, hittin' the girls on the ass and pushing people out his way. Besides the usual drunks I hadn't had no problems with anybody for six months. But this nigga was carryin' on like he didn't have a good brain in his head, and when the manager gave me the signal I sure enough tossed him out on his ass. He took out a knife but he didn't know how to use it and I got it from him before he could really do anything. So the dude runs down the street screaming that he was gonna get me.

"I was from Southeast, and if he wanted a fight I would have been glad to give him one. But he was running away, so I just took him for a chump and went back inside. The club closed about two hours after that, and when I came out to go home the street was empty. So I got in my car and started drivin'. I didn't notice that there was a car fol-lowin' me until I was on the other side of the river, and then I just thought it was some cops in an unmarked tryin' to mess with me 'cuz it was four in the morning on a Tues-day night. But when I parked the car in front of my build-ing they parked too.

"So I just went in the building. I still had my .45 from the service in the house, and I was gonna come out and scare them. We lived on the ground floor, so it only took a second to get in the house. Your mother was in the living room next to the window tryin' to get you back to sleep, and I made the mistake of turnin' the living room light on. You started cryin' and your mama turned to curse at me and the next thing I knew I heard the glass breakin' and your mama was on the floor and you were cryin' even louder.

"I ran to the window to see the mothafucka from earlier in the night standing outside the window with a pistol in his hand turning to walk back to his car. He'd seen your mama's silhouette and thought it was me. God had it the bullets missed you altogether. I called an ambulance. She died at the hospital. I was so busy lookin' after you and your mama until the ambulance came that I let him get away.

"And the whole thing was that if I hadn't taken that damn job like she had begged me not to do I wouldn't have been in that position. It turned out that that dude was some young heroin dealer from some other neighborhood that wanted to prove that nobody should fuck wit' him. If I just hadn't gone in the house your mama would be tellin' you this story instead of me."

He finally paused. I heard the tears clogging his voice and I felt my own gathering.

"I was just gonna go pull out the gun and scare 'em. Hell, it was 1978. People wasn't getting shot like that, out of the blue and for no reason. Now it happen every day, but back then it made the papers and everything.

"Your mama didn't have no family besides her grandma, and her grandma was real old and out of her mind over in St. Elizabeths. Her parents had got killed in the U Street riots when she was real little. Didn't even have a lot of friends. But she was so beautiful, always smilin', always had something to say, just wantin' us to get married and get a house. You and me was all she had."

"So that's—"

"I ain't done, son. Day of the funeral I left you with my mother. She was still livin' then, and I went over in Shaw, over behind Dunbar near Rhode Island. That was where his spot was. Plenty of people had told me, because he was runnin' around proud that what he did had gotten in the paper. He thought he was the man. And I remember he was just standin' there in front of the buildin'. His boys had gone inside for a minute. All I needed was a minute. All I had was my knife and all I heard when I walked away was the sound of him choking while he bled to death through his neck. I did it in the war and I told myself that it wasn't any different.

"But you know it didn't change anything. When I was walkin' down that dark alley back to my car I realized that dark cuttin' his throat didn't do a damn thing for me or you. What we had was already gone. God hadn't meant for her to stay, and if she had, who knows. Maybe I might have broke her heart. Maybe I mighta stop her from doin' what she really wanted to do. I don't know, son. I guess I'm sayin' all this because I never told anybody. Cops ain't ask no questions. To them somebody had done the neighborhood a favor.

"And you know right after I did it I came over to my mama's and I got you. You looked just like her to me. And while I was holdin' you that night I realized that it was all up to me what happened to you. Every action I took would have something to do with you and I couldn't just react anymore. You know in life we only here for a minute and when the clock runs out we ain't got nothin' left but what we've done and what we remember and what we leave behind us.

"People look at me and they see a bartender who never graduated from high school, who joined the Army at seventeen and went and fought in a white man's war against people who I didn't have no problems with. They just see somebody who makes drinks. But I know I got a son who's gonna do way more than his old man. All he has to do is use his head and he can make whatever he wants happen. Look, I know I've said all of this at one time and you might not want to talk to me or you might wanna get away from me altogether, but the one thing I need you to know is that I love you more than anything in this world."

"I love you too, Pop," I replied.

It was a confession that surpassed anything that had ever crossed my ears. I sat there with that phone to my ear listening as a son and a friend. As the son I had more questions than there was room for. As a friend I wanted to put my arm around him and drive us away from our current location. I had forced him to look at things he had tried to drown in gin and orange juice for my whole life. This was the demon that made him alienate friends and live a life without anybody.

Then there was his revenge, as planned and calculated as a crime but as human as breathing in and out. As he told the tale he had taken me to a place I shouldn't have been. I tried to drift into his trance and cram myself between the arms of that bullet-wounded woman I didn't remember. But I couldn't. Where I had an empty void he had a photo album of the things love was made of.

"Pop?"

"Yeah, son?"

"Were you ever gonna tell me if I didn't ask?" His pause echoed through the phone. I squatted on the cool ground and stretched the receiver's cord to its limit.

"Every time you asked I told myself the next time. Now you nineteen and I'm fifty-four and I ain't never told you nothin' 'bout your mama. Locked all her things up in the attic. Then I locked the attic. That's why the house is so cold in the winter, 'cuz I ain't been up there to put in insulation since your grandma died and we moved in the house when you was five. Delilah'd probably kick my ass right now if she could."

He giggled, and then it rumbled into a laugh. I laughed with him, because I didn't want him to be alone.

"You know your mama was gonna be a lawyer. She went to college and then she was in law school for a while till she got pregnant. When she was studying she used to tape up the

dark

181

names of cases all around the apartment and she would lay on the sofa and close her eyes and walk around with her eyes closed. When she remembered a case she would walk over to where it was taped up and look at it. If she was right she balled up the name and threw it away. It ain't make no sense to me, but you know me. If it don't come in a bottle I don't know nothin' about it."

"You know a lot. You raised me, didn't you?"

"That ain't got nothin' to do wit' knowin'. That's about doin'. I did what I needed to to make sure that you were all right. That ain't mean I knew anything about it. I'm not done with you yet. You're never done being a father. That's what I try and tell Ray Ray every time he comes over here to the house with Brianna. When that girl grows up, only thing that gonna change for him is the kind of problems he gotta deal wit'. Up until the day you die you gotta show your kids how to do somethin'. There's always somethin' they don't know how to do."

"Did you love her?"

"Your mama? More than anything. But look, son, why don't you come home. We got a lot we need to talk about."

"I'll be back on Tuesday, Pop. Got some things I gotta do first."

"Well like I said before, you grown now. If you need anything . . ."

"Yeah, I'll call you. I love you, Pop."

"I love you too, son."

I dropped the receiver fast and started walking towards

the city. I had forty dollars in my pocket. But I couldn't find a cabbie who'd let me spend it. My body screamed for a Newport. My jaw was a loud soreness that gave me a headache. But I kept walking, past a huge construction area and a sports arena and a camera store, until I found myself seated on the railing next to 77 watching cars pass down the straightaway. I sat there and hummed a church song I couldn't remember the words to until I caught my breath.

Nick would never have such a heart-to-heart with his old man, nor would he ever leave the city to visit Charlotte. He would never learn the truth about his long-lost mother. In short, he would never again have life. Unlike money or material things I had taken the one thing I couldn't give back. And no matter what I did or didn't get away with, that was never going to change. Being a man meant I had to stare Nick in the face every day for the rest of my life.

After a while I maneuvered my way across the freeway until I was back in downtown. It was three-fifteen. By the time I got back to the building it was close to four.

E was posted on the front steps like a military guard. He paced back and forth across the stoop armed with nothing but his cellular, a lit cigarette, and a worried look on his face.

"You look like somebody told you I died!" I yelled at him. E's head snapped in my direction. His eyes widened in surprise and relief.

"What happened?" he asked as he walked over and gave me a half-hug.

"Me? What happened to you?" I asked plainly. "Thought

you was supposed to have my back. It was like five dudes outside I had to fight by myself." I didn't have a single doubt that he had had my back. I just wanted to hear what his story was.

"Man, by the time I got over there you was gone. I ain't even know it was you till Alicia told me."

"Yeah, she stood there and watched it all happen."

"You got your ass whipped?" He grinned.

"I hit him a couple times. He hit me and I ran. Wasn't no way I was beatin' him." I rubbed my jaw even though it made it hurt more.

"But you all right?" E asked again.

"My jaw hurt like hell but I'ma be all right."

"So you got your first ass-whuppin', huh?"

I had to smile despite the fact that that made my jaw hurt too. "You had said it was comin' one day, didn't you?"

"You take Yvette and Alicia home?"

"Alicia went home wit' the man who beat your ass."

"What we standing down here for?" My feet ached from walking for so long.

"I don't know. Let's go upstairs."

With a newly lit cigarette between my lips I wrapped some ice cubes in my bath towel and pressed them against my jaw. The chill soothed all the way down to the bone. E had turned all the lights on at four in the morning and it made the apartment seem smaller. The darkness gave it more space. By the time my cigarette had burned halfway he had changed the subject.

"So where's this broad you was tellin' me about?" he asked. "She live on this floor?"

"Yeah, down the hall."

"You think she home?"

"Nah. When she home she leaves me a note."

"A note? Like you Denzel or somebody."

"Hey, I get mine."

"Since when? You ain't get no ass till you was sixteen, and if it hadn't been for Sierra you wouldn't have got none after that."

"Whatever, man," I said, scowling.

"Aw man, don't get mad. Look, I'll stop messin' wit' you about it. Believe me man, broads don't bring you nothin' but problems. You remember all the broads I used to have?"

Like I told you, E was the lucky one. He could just walk up to a girl and ask her for her number and he'd get it. He didn't have to be dressed up or use lines or anything. Maybe it had to do with the fact that he had straight hair and slanted eyes and girls around our way didn't see that too often. Maybe unlike me he didn't take it all so seriously. Maybe he was just lucky. After all, his mom hadn't been shot through a window.

"I talked to Ray Ray," I said as I crushed my cigarette butt in the ashtray.

"For real? What was he talkin' about?" E asked as he handed me a new smoke and lit the last one for himself.

"Snow and Cuckoo got shot in front of the carry-out." dark

"They dead?" he asked fearfully.

"Nah, bullet broke Snow's arm and Cuckoo took a few but he supposed to be all right."

"Good. Hope they took that damn mark off his face when they fixed his arm," E said.

He got the name Snowflake in the fourth grade because of the birthmark on the right side of his cheek. It was a tan spot on his golden-brown complexion. Calvin Middleton lost a permanent tooth for calling him that name and he became known as Snagglepuss until high school when he got it fixed. Now thirteen years later the name Snowflake still stuck as he walked the streets with one arm in a cast looking for a blue Maxima wagon and whoever had shot him.

E always made jokes about the birthmark that looked like a snowflake. But he never said them around Snow because he knew better than to bring it up to his face. It wasn't ugly or anything, but it got your attention. That was what made it suit him, because he was the same way. Snow was quiet and subtle but he knew how to get your attention.

"So you know what Snow want to do," I said.

"Shoot until he hits somethin'," E replied while he searched the empty refrigerator.

"You know it. Ray Ray said he be walkin' all around the neighborhood lookin' for the Maxima the dudes was in."

"Is that supposed to surprise me?" he asked, looking at his watch. "But look man, I gotta go to church in the morning. Ma said I ain't been in two weeks. Wanna go with us?"

I paused and thought about the hard seats and the big ladies with big hats and the preacher sweating like a cooked pig after his sermon. I was sure that I would pass. But then I thought about my mama, and how God had given her enough life to get me into the world before He took her home. God had saved me from the Terminator and from jail. I hoped. The least I could do was listen to what He had to say.

sunday

Pass me not O gentle Savior/Hear my humble cry/While on others thou art calling/Do not pass me by.

I had heard the song before but never that fast. It was as if the entire choir was a 33 record singing at 45. The drummer's arms looked like they were about to fly off and the piano player rocketed through notes and measures like a bowling ball through pins. Members of the congregation clapped and jumped up and stomped their feet against the carpeted floor while I was perfectly still.

It was the Holy Ghost and I hadn't seen Him at work in a long time.

The choir wailed as if Gabriel's trumpet had sounded and they were singing their last song before the Rapture. If I wasn't feeling what was going on around me, did that mean that I was going to hell? E wasn't feeling it either and neither were many of the younger people in the sanctuary. We all just watched the scene unfold like it was on a movie screen or something we had viewed through a bus window while it was heading in the opposite direction.

Pass me not O gentle Savior/Hear my humble cry/While on others thou art calling/Do not pass me by.

E's mama popped out of her seat like a jack-in-the-box, her dress flailing in front of our faces as she began a circular spin that turned her orange-and-maroon fabric into a spinning pinwheel.

"Thank you Jesus!" she shouted, her Indian accent very apparent. Two women in the row in front of us stood up and clapped for her as she spun. Three more emerged from the row behind. I assumed the church was used to it, seeing a woman who should have had a dot on her forehead catching the Holy Ghost. But they were brothers and sisters in the Lord, and among them I guess she'd found her place. That college roommate of hers must have been very convincing. But if she hadn't been my best friend's mother I probably would have snickered.

Then the volume slowly faded. Ms. Mehdi's spin settled

d a r k

into left and right turns and then she stopped, just in time for the head deacon to announce that it was time for offering.

I had been to plenty of churches before. From age seven to sixteen I was always invited by every friend's mama to experience the Lord. Pop said his grace at meals and we said prayers at night, but he never went to church. I couldn't see Pop in a church. He told me that if I wanted to go to church that was a choice *I* had to make. He was my father but God was supposed to handle the religion department. So I had spent years going to church once every other month. It had always been a different church, but with the same people sitting in the pews. Somewhere deep inside I thought that a lot of them weren't there because they wanted to be, that we were all just going through the motions.

Still, I knew in my heart that God was watching over me. At a party shots had gone through a basement window I had stood in front of seconds earlier. My train would come rushing into the station when the wrong group of dudes on the platform were looking at me like they were about to start something. Money I needed came out of nowhere, or Snow escaped getting locked up again. I always won my fights. It was things like that that had let me know that God was watching. I always kept that in the back of my mind, even after what happened with Nick.

General offering began, and when the usher told us it was our turn we hokey-pokeyed up the aisle, dropped our money in the plate, and went down the other aisle back to our seats. On the way we exchanged smiles and greetings, as if we were really a part of it. I wondered if they would have smiled the same way had they seen me with Ray's Beretta in my shorts a few nights before, or if they had seen me hop in the back of Snow's wagon and drive away from Nick's body with a smoking gun in my hand. All the church people I had known didn't want to know me. They just wanted someone else to socialize with. I hadn't come to church to socialize.

I took my seat and looked around me at the place where God was supposed to live. He knew what I was thinking and feeling. He knew why I had pulled the trigger and He definitely knew that I was sorry. But I didn't know if that was enough. The offering cycle was completed and after a ten-minute prayer by one of the deacons the choir led us into one last song before the sermon.

I'm on the battlefield for my Lord/Yes I'm on the battlefield for my Lord/And I promise him that I/will serve him till I die/I'm on the battlefield for my Lord.

As I listened I imagined the dudes on my block gunning down their enemies in the name of the Lord, and it didn't take me too long to figure out that that wasn't what the song was about. The battle the song talked about was one between good and evil. God and the Devil fought every day, and if you were on the battlefield for the Lord then you were a good guy. I didn't know if I had ever fought at all. I had always just gone with what I felt. I never wanted to steal anything. I had never wanted to hurt anyone, so I didn't, except

dark

191

for when I had to defend myself. But I had told lies. I had lied to my father about killing. Two sins in the same sentence. And all it took was one sin to keep you out of heaven. At least that was what I had always heard.

The preacher approached the pulpit.

"Morning, church," he said with a grim look on his face. The church responded to him. He was a short, blue-black, balding man with no neck, and his robe seemed too big for him. But there was something in his voice that made everything else about him insignificant. He had the voice of the Lord waiting in the back of his throat.

"You know, Sister Walker and I were watchin' the news just last night and they said that fifteen black boys had been killed in the last thirty days. You know, that's a boy every other day. And they're dyin' by other boys' hands, other boys wit' guns who don't know nothin' 'bout the life the Lord gave them." The church yessed and amened.

"Every other day in one month some black boy was killed at the hands of his own brother. Now can you imagine goin' to your house every night and havin' to worry that while you slept your own brother might kill you?" Some of the congregation amened and others outright said no. I remained silent.

"You see, the problem with too many of our youth today is that when they think of home, they just think about the place where they lay their heads. They don't think about the streets they walk on, the schools they go to, the places where they eat or anything else. The neighbors across the street and the storeowner on the corner and even their friends ain't their family. If Mama or Daddy ain't got nothin' to say about it, then that means they don't have to listen to nobody else. And see, when they think about that and they get these guns and shoot another boy over drugs or a coat or some little girl, they don't see that they're killin' their own family."

"That's right!" a deaconess shouted as she raised her right hand in the air.

"And some of them might live just across from this church or down the street. Some of these brothers that have killed their brothers just might be sitting in this church right now. And if they are there's a little something that they need to hear." He paused and opened the thick pulpit Bible to a marked page. "Please turn to I John 3:14–16. It reads:

"'He that loveth not his brother abideth in death. Whosoever hateth his brother is a murderer: and ye know that no murderer hath eternal life abiding in him. Hereby perceive we the love of God, because he laid down his life for us: and we ought to lay down our lives for the brethren.'"

The preacher went on. With every sentence he planted spiritual seeds he hoped might sprout deep within our souls. It was his job to show the wrong the right and lead the blind out of the darkness. As his words dug deeper into my conscience, sweat gathered on his ample forehead and then cascaded down his dark face. He moved back and forth behind the pulpit like a performer on a stage. Twenty minutes later he brought his work to a finish when five people got the dark Holy Ghost and danced wildly in the pews.

By the end he had me too. God had me. But not in the

same way. I was still back at his reading of the text and that word "murderer." I was a murderer and not a killer. I was to have no eternal life. Neither would Snow, or Alicia, or my own father. We should have laid down our anger and even our lives for our brothers. I should have laid down my life for Nick.

It was one thing to say I had shot him or popped him or put him in a black bag, but being a "murderer" struck me as something altogether different, something much more evil. It had just taken that one step. Now the Bible and the preacher said that I couldn't go to heaven and there was nothing I could do about it.

> Come to Jesus/Come to Jesus/Just now/Come to Jesus/ Come to Jesus/Just now.

The preacher beckoned the congregation to its feet as he made his appeal to those who wanted to be saved. I wanted to be saved, but not just by getting dunked in a pool of water and being called Brother Williams the next time I came to Charlotte. I didn't just want to read Bible verses and put on a suit every Sunday morning so that things could be all right. That alone wasn't going to express-mail me to the pearly gates, and I knew that that was all the preacher could give me.

I wanted back whatever I had lost in Sierra's doorway when I witnessed my first instance of betrayal. I might have been a murderer, but walking up that aisle to the preacher wasn't going to fix my crime. A baptism could not bring

Nick back or erase my crime. That act was a part of me and it would follow me back to the crime scene in the morning.

"you all right, man?"

E asked me as the congregation funneled out of the sanctuary. Church was over.

I hadn't left my seat since general offering and my eyes were staring past the pew in front of me at my mother lying in the dark on the living room floor, clutching onto me and the last moments of her life. Like father, like son. Pop and I had both sought refuge from our pain in the greatest sin of all.

"You all right?" E asked me again.

"Life is crazy," I said blankly.

"What you talkin 'bout?"

"It's just real easy to get caught up," I said as I rubbed my temples. I had a headache from only getting four hours' sleep. "Just listenin' to the preacher—"

"Hey," he interjected as he sat back down next to me, "I hope you ain't beatin' yourself up about the preacher's sermon and all. All you can do now is pray."

"You ain't the one that did it," I said. "You ain't see that look he had on his face right before I shot him."

"He shot at you."

"That ain't make it right," I said. "But I gotta live wit' that my mama's dead too."

"What?"

"I talked to Pop last night. My mama died when I was

dark

195

three months old. There's more, but I ain't even ready to tell you."

"I'm sorry."

"Don't be sorry, man. Shoot, when we was younger all we wanted to know was where our mamas were. I think I always knew she wasn't never comin' back, but I just wanted to know why. And now I know. It's time for me to go back home."

"You sure?"

"Between Snow and Cuckoo and Pop I got to."

"They all grown men. And one of 'em put a gun in your hand that you killed somebody with."

"What you tryin' to say? You act like they ain't your boys too."

"I'm tryin' to say that you always been the smart one. Figure it out for yourself. If you wanna talk about God you ain't down here sittin' in this church livin' in my mama's apartment buildin' because you want to. You ain't meet none of the people you met just because it happened. God got a plan for everybody. You hadn't never left DC in your life, and I think now you know it's a whole world out there if you wanna see it. You always said you wanted to go to college and all that. You can go down here."

"I can go up there too," I said. "But I don't know about Pop."

"Your Pops was all right before you was born. If he was in a wheelchair or had cancer or somethin' like that I could see why you was worried, but he got a job just like you. I ain't wanna say nothin' to you before, but your life ain't about Snow and Ray Ray. It's about you and what you wanna do wit' it. Now I know you been through way more than me in this last year, but you my boy. Nah, you my family. All the months since I left the neighborhood and I been living here and learnin', I was tryin' to think of a way to help you come down."

"It's the same problems everywhere if you black," I said.

"Yeah, but at least when you're somewhere new there's new ways to deal wit' 'em. I ain't tryin' to press you 'bout nothin', man. But when I was doin' stupid stuff you was always the one to stop me and tell me what was up. I'm just tryin' to do the same thing."

"I know," I said. "You my family too, and I love you like my brother. I know somethin's gotta change, but I gotta figure out what it is for myself. What you about to do, anyway?"

"Mama got dinner cooked at the house. You wanna eat?"

"You know it," I said. "But let me get a few minutes alone before we go."

"All right," he said with a degree of surprise. "I'll be out front."

When the swinging exit doors swung closed behind him I looked around the empty church and felt relieved. The only eyes watching me were His. I knew that He was there, just like the air or the atoms and molecules that make up everything in the world. And when I closed my eyes and meditated I felt Him in my head listening to everything I had to say. He gave me something at the end of that prayer and He took something away at the same time.

They had said in science class that change was a constant but that nothing was ever really created or destroyed. In less than two weeks, God had plugged in all of the missing pieces to an old puzzle and presented me with an entirely new one. I wasn't quite sure of where to start, but I knew that it was a puzzle I had to solve on my own.

"do you eat fish, thai?"

Ms. Mehdi yelled from the kitchen.

"Yes, ma'am," I replied. She had changed into some sweatpants and a T-shirt and was warming up the dinner she had cooked the night before. I was stuck with the image of her catching the Holy Ghost. She was Indian. It didn't seem to fit. But at the same time it did.

E and I were watching *Friday* for the hundredth time in the living room. Ice Cube once again threw down with a man bigger and stronger than he was and was almost willing to end that man's life to end his reign of terror. It made me think about Diamelo the Terminator and how my fight scene didn't last nearly as long. *Friday* was one of the last movies we had gone to see before E had left, and watching it was one of those things that made me forget that I was five hundred miles from home sitting on the sofa of a woman who I used to hate.

I had despised Ms. Mehdi. She had just popped up out of nowhere and tried to be a mother to her child. I was sitting there when she walked through the door to their apartment and said hello to all of us, like she was trying to sell us Mary

Kay or some *Watchtowers*. She had been the missing gear in E's machine for his whole life, and she thought she could just pop back in and make everything okay again. That wasn't right. Somebody should have made her suffer for what she did. But on the way to E's house I had learned that she had suffered already.

She had come to America at eighteen. She somehow got the money and the permission to use it at a time when it should have been impossible. Her mother had died and she felt like she needed to make her own way. She didn't fit into her culture, into the role she was supposed to play and the things she was supposed to believe in. So she came to DC with a thousand dollars, a visa, and not much else.

She got a job in the gift shop at the Museum of Natural History downtown, where E's dad was working as a maintenance man. He asked her out mainly out of curiosity, and before he knew it they were living together. She found him to be the nicest man she'd ever met, and considering her collegiate exposure to blackness I imagined that she might not have seen it as that big of a deal. But a black-and-Indian relationship was more than a little wild for 1977. When E was born there were more problems. There were questions about how E might be brought up and about the marriage and everything else. She actually had a breakdown and literally disappeared. It was after that breakdown E's dad had started drinking, apparently for the first time in his life.

During her disappearance, Ms. Mehdi got her full citizenship and went to Detroit and Atlanta and then to Charlotte, where a late-night infomercial introduced her to real estate. So after three years of odd jobs and of getting established, and with the luck of having a building left to her, she came back for her son.

E had told me the story like he was reading it out of a book. He didn't mention how he felt or if he loved her or anything. But when I watched the way they interacted it was like one year had made the past eighteen unimportant. They kissed and hugged and laughed and joked like she had thrown him birthday parties and held him on her lap since birth. But no matter how much I wanted to know what that felt like I now knew that I never would.

Somewhere in my four hours of sleep the night before I had dreamt that I was in my faceless mother's arms standing in the living room of my father's house. Her touch made me feel safer than I ever had before.

She kept whispering, "What you have is always more important than what you don't." She said it over and over again until my alarm went off.

"Time to eat!" Ms. Mehdi yelled from the kitchen.

E sprung up like he hadn't had the combo meal from Mickey D's on the way in. But I took my time. I loved collard greens, but as far as the Indian food part was concerned I was a little skeptical. But I had to admit that it smelled good.

The kitchen was a cloud of curry, fish, and rice with Ms. Mehdi right in the middle.

"Don't give me that look," she said to me as I slowly inched toward the plate she had prepared for me.

"What look you talkin' 'bout?" I asked.

"That 'I don't think I'm going to like this' look."

"I just never had Indian food before, that's all."

"I don't even know why you fakin' like that," E said with his mouthful of greens. "Ma's food be tight to death."

"All right," I said as I took the plate closest to me from the counter along with a glass of fruit punch. By the time I followed E back into the living room the credits were rolling on *Friday*. E pushed stop and put in *Deep Cover*, another one of our favorites. We inhaled our plates, went back for more, and inhaled them again. By the time 4:00 P.M. hit we were both asleep on the couch with a severe case of black people sickness.

"thai? thai?"

Ms. Mehdi's voice cracked through my subconscious and broke off my dream about Robin and getting down in her shower. My eyes slid open like elevator doors. With the same clothes and the same smile, she sat across from me like a patient teacher waiting for full attention from a student.

"So I hear you're leaving tomorrow."

"Yeah," I said groggily. "Gotta get back to work."

"I understand that," she said. "I guess we never really got a chance to talk since you've been here."

"It's all right. I mean I know you been busy with work and all. But thank you for givin' me a place to stay and everything."

"It's no problem. I've been having some trouble renting

all the units on that floor anyway. I don't know what it is, but I'll get some people in there as soon as all the college kids come back."

"Where'd E go?" I asked, noticing his absence.

"Upstairs to run his mouth with Yvette. I'm glad I got him his own line or else I'd never get to make any calls around here."

"I hear you," I said.

"So what are you trying to do with yourself?" She asked it in that friend-of-the-family/high-school-guidance-counselor way that always made me feel nervous, as if I wasn't doing what it took to live up to my potential.

"What do you mean?" Playing ignorant was always the best policy in situations like that.

"Enrique says that you were thinking about going to college."

"Yeah, I'm goin'." I visualized the UDC registration packet on my desk that I had never opened. "I just want to make some money first."

"You can always make money, but the more time you spend just making money the harder it is to take time out to get your education. I've had a lot of friends who were caught up that way."

"I know, but I don't feel—"

"You said you were thinking about real estate."

"My dad always talks about it, and I want to help him when he gets his license—"

"Did you know you could learn what you need to get your own license in a few months and you can take the classes even while you're working full-time? You don't even need a college degree to sell real estate."

"For real? I always thought that you did," I said. With all my talk about going into real estate with Pop I had never known how easy it actually was. "But how much does it cost?"

"It depends. Classes can be a few hundred, maybe a thousand or two at the most. From what I understand, it costs less here in Charlotte than it does up in the District."

"Well I don't know about stayin' in Charlotte."

"Why not?"

"This ain't where I live. I don't think I can just up and move. I gotta make sure my pops is all right."

"I'm sure that your father was taking care of himself before you were born. I think that he'd be okay with doing it again."

"It's still something I have to think about," I said.

She laughed softly. "I can see why you and Enrique are such good friends. You two are just alike. He had all the same reasons for not coming down to live with me, besides the fact that he hadn't seen his mother since before he could remember. He didn't want to start anything new and he didn't want to leave that neighborhood of yours. But after thinking about it he realized that he wanted a change and that I could give him what he needed. You know, in the year he's been here all he's talked about is you coming down, how he wanted to share everything he learned with you."

I thought about the monthly phone calls where E would explain how different things were and how I had to come and visit. I had always turned him down. I didn't like making trips. I didn't like being in places where I didn't know the streets or the people who walked them. I didn't even like going uptown. Neither did Ray Ray and Snow. That was why we did the same things night after night and weekend after weekend, because we were afraid that the earth was flat outside of the DC city limits. If we traveled past Silver Spring we might slip and fall off. E's leaving had changed our world like Columbus or Magellan had changed theirs. His going somewhere else and staying there opened up a whole new world of possibilities none of us wanted to deal with. Up until then anything we needed was less than ten minutes away on foot. We didn't need to go anywhere else. Nobody on Shaw liked change, especially not Mr. Mitchell.

"What did Mr. Mitchell say to you when you wanted to take E to Charlotte?" It was a question I didn't have the right to ask but I took the privilege anyway.

"You have to understand that Enrique's father and I have a very strange relationship. I don't think that either of us has ever loved the way we loved each other. But love isn't enough sometimes. Other things get in the way. And even when things didn't work out our love and our trust didn't change. I had to leave. I can't really explain why, but the Lord told me to. And when I came back all those years later I think I had something both he and Enrique needed in their lives. I guess the bottom line was that even after everything he still trusted me and he knows that for right now Enrique is better off far away from Shaw. He knows that the best thing was to let his son go, even if it's only for a little while. But I have not kidnapped my son. His father talks to him twice a week and he's supposed to come down for his vacation at the end of September."

Mr. Mitchell was a quiet man. He went to work, came home, paid the bills as best he could, and went to sleep in between. He said hello, goodbye, and how you doing, but he didn't want to know much else. Maybe he felt like he couldn't afford to worry about other people's problems. Maybe he didn't like people altogether. But he always welcomed me into his house and that was all that I could ask for.

Every once in a while he and Pop would sit out on our porch in the summer and talk for an hour or two about things and people I didn't know about, and then they would walk off down O Street and blend into the scenery. And that was all I knew. Maybe that was all there was to know. But Ms. Mehdi gave me the idea that once upon a time there had been a lot more, something that her departure might have closed off forever.

Now she was talking to me about the future and my best friend's future and how she wanted them to be intertwined in Charlotte. She didn't know that I was a killer or that my girl had lost our baby or that my mother had died right after I was born or that my dad thought he was a killer too or that my jaw ached from a right hook from Arnold Schwarzenegger's stunt double.

If she had known, would she still want to help me? Would it even matter to her? I didn't want to owe anybody anything, since I already had a debt I couldn't pay back anywhere on earth.

Silence hung in the living room air like the smell of curry from dinner. I didn't know what to say but I knew that the conversation wasn't over even if I was going home in the morning.

"If you did want to stay I'm sure we could work something out with the apartment. I could even get you something at a realty company while you took your classes."

The expression on my face was as blank as unlined paper. She didn't know me but she wanted to take me away from everything. She wanted to pull out of that alley where Nick's corpse was rotting in my mind and into the seat of my own periwinkle 4Runner with a five-disc CD changer, and I just didn't know about it. I was a killer who was about to go back to filing documents in a hot-ass office on D Street. I was going back to my block, where one friend was walking around with a broken arm and a pistol looking for a car with a make and model that every other dude drove. I was going back to drinking beer in front of Ray Ray's building and waiting to find out who would get killed before the summer was over. I was absolutely positively sure that I was going back while I was turning away from what could have been my brightest future. I didn't let that bother me. Pop had always told me to think things through and look at all the possibilities. That's what I was doing.

"It's a big decision to be makin'," I said in a confused voice.

"Oh, dear, I know it is. I don't want you to just up and answer right now. You've got that look on your face like you don't know which way is up and you think that there's something that I'm not telling you. Enrique gave me that same look. Just in case you're wondering, I know how hard it was when Enrique left you to move here. I know your mother wasn't around while you grew up either.

"And I can't lie to you, the first three months with him here in Charlotte were really hard. Once he got down here he had so many questions and I couldn't give him the answers he wanted. Sometimes he'd leave in the jeep and not come back for two days or he'd call me from a pay phone somewhere because he'd driven angrily in no particular direction until he got lost. One time he got all the way to South Carolina. I had helped him to leave what he knew, and learning everything all over again at eighteen was really hard. He didn't know the streets or the neighborhoods, and worst of all he didn't know me and he hadn't known me for his whole life. I remember one time he started throwing all my dishes against the wall. But the Lord had it that in time it worked, and well, I'll just say this and I won't say any more. I know that if I help you now, you will help me when the time comes. That's why I'm offering you this, because I can and because the Lord told me that I should. You've got our number, so if you want to do it just give me a call, okay?"

I nodded as I stood to my feet in my wrinkled khakis and shirt and borrowed tie. In my mind I stood in front of the broken living room window in the Southeast apartment. I wondered if my mother was this easy to talk to, if I could have told her about Sierra and Nick. What would her advice have been? Could she have stopped me from punching Nick's clock? Or would she have just brought me cookies

dark

207

while I was doing my bid in Lorton? Were there photos of her in the attic? I had to check if I ever made it back to the house.

"You okay?" Ms. Mehdi asked me as I walked toward the front door.

"Uh-huh," I mumbled as I fiddled with the doorknob to exit. "Got a lot on my mind, if you know what I mean."

"Of course. Don't you want to say goodbye to Enrique?"

"I'll see him before I leave," I said as I got the door open. The thick humid air pressed against my face as I walked through the doorframe.

By the time I got to my car I barely remembered where I was or whose house I was leaving or even what city I was in. I had been away from Shaw for almost a week and I had a brain filled to the brim with questions. Should I have just stayed in DC like Snowflake had said? I didn't know. But Snow was too far in to take advice from.

in the car

2Pac announced that it was "him against the world" as I parked in front of the building for one of the last times. Ms. Mehdi's offer hung around my neck like a bag of cinder blocks. I looked for Robin's car but I didn't see it. I was leaving in the morning but I couldn't leave without seeing her. One last time would finish it. As I climbed the steps I told myself that I would leave a note on her door so she would come over as soon as she got in. But as I reached the top of the stairs Robin slid to the back burner.

Alicia, the root of my sore jaw, sat cross-legged in front of my door with her face in her hands. She had on the same clothes from the night before and her hair was a mess. But she didn't look hurt.

"What the fuck are you doin' here?" I almost yelled.

"Waitin' for you," she said calmly. "I wanted to talk to you."

"Look, 'Licia. I don't know what kind of fuckin' game you playin' but I don't want no part of it. He was tryin' to kill me last night."

"Nah, he wasn't gonna kill you," she said nonchalantly. "He might have kicked your ass but he wasn't gonna kill you. He ain't no killer."

"You can say that shit calmly because it wasn't your ass that was running through the woods to get away from him. Besides, you should know that anybody can be a killer."

"You have no idea what happened last night. I pretty much had to run out of his apartment and into a cab at four in the mornin' so he wouldn't beat me to death while I slept."

"You brought that on yourself and it ain't my problem. I'm leavin' tomorrow and I don't need to get into nothing else with nobody."

"Thai, I ain't come here to get you jumped again. I ain't go to the club to get you jumped either. Once upon a time I thought we was supposed to be friends. I came all the way out here to say I'm sorry about what happened. I didn't even know that he was gonna be there last night."

"That don't make no difference. First you say you ain't trippin' about what he thinks or what he thinks about what

dark

209

you do. But after I drop you off I come back home and somebody's waitin' in my hall to hit me in the face. You say you goin' for a free ride on him but the next time I'm wit' you in the club somebody else runs up on me when I'm dancin' and then I'm fightin' with your boyfriend outside. The bottom line about it is that no matter how much you don't care about him I take the ass-whippin' he should be givin' you! And see, what he don't know is I fight back! I ain't gotta fight with my fists either!"

"Look, like I said, I'm sorry. Can I just come in for a minute and charge my cell phone so I can call a cab? My battery died last night and the bus don't run too good on Sunday nights."

"Yeah, whatever. But as soon as that cab come you got to go," I said, wanting to kick myself for letting her in.

"Fine," she replied as she stood up and cleared the doorway so I could put my key in. I twisted the locks open and we entered. But as I crossed the doorframe my anger dribbled off and I began to wonder where she had been hiding since her escape from his apartment. She plugged her phone charger into the outlet next to the door and placed her phone inside.

"So what happened? Where'd you stay last night?" I plopped myself on the sofa. She sat on the other end and stared at the front door.

"After you got into the fight I came outside to see what had happened. Enrique and Yvette came behind me but Diamelo saw me and just grabbed me by the arm and made me get into his car with him. We didn't say anything to each other all the way to his house. He drove up to his building and told me that I better still be in the apartment when he came back, so I did what he said. But while I was waitin' I got tired and fell asleep. Like two hours later he came in and started yelling and we got into a fight about me and you and I was trying to tell him we was friends and he started throwin' stuff and smashin' things and then he left again. I didn't feel safe being there anymore.

"So I scraped together my last little bit of money I had before my check tomorrow and I called a cab. But before the cab got there he came back again and trashed the place some more. As soon as I saw the cab I ran out and got in. Cab took me to the Amtrak station, and I went to sleep there for a couple hours until it was time for me to go to work. When I got off work I wanted to come here to apologize. I ain't got too many friends, so I like to keep them when I can."

There was truth in her face. She was eighteen, and while her goal was to juice her man for as much as she could while keeping some of her freedom she hadn't expected it all to go the way it had. She didn't know what women can make men do. In the beginning I had wanted her but now I felt sorry for even walking up to her at the party and speaking in the first place. It was something I didn't need with all the things that had my own future hanging in the balance. It would no longer be part of the equation when my belongings and I hit Interstate 85 in the morning.

dark

"I don't think you should be with him no more," I said.

"Yeah, tell me something I don't already know. I hadn't never seen him like he was last night. He was crazy. He could've killed me if he wanted to."

"He probably could have," I said coldly, remembering that a few minutes earlier she had sworn that he wouldn't have taken my life. "Anybody can kill if you push them far enough."

"Somebody ever push you too far?" she asked.

"Yeah," I said, hoping there would be no follow-up question.

"Would you do it again?"

"Hell nah. But it's a lot of stuff I wouldn't do again." I drew one of the last four Newports from the pack on the coffee table and lit it. "I wouldn't have started smokin'. I wouldn't have got my girl pregnant. Just mistakes I made."

She let out a deep sigh. "I guess everybody got their little demons that they gotta live with," she said.

"Yeah, mine be flying around my head laughin' at me, saying, 'Thai, you ain't shit! Thai, you always fuckin' up!' "

She giggled.

"You think that's funny?"

"Nah, you just talk like you so old when you nineteen. You did whatever you did and it's done. You need to get over it."

"You can't just get over killin' somebody. You need to get over actin' like you always in control and you not. Even if you ain't gonna admit it to me I know your nigga got you on the run."

"You right, but—"

"Look, your phone charged yet?"

She peeked over and saw that it was charged enough for a short call. "Yeah, I almost forgot." I wondered if she even had cab fare or if she was really trying to weasel her way into laying low at Apartment 3C for the night. I came to the conclusion that I didn't care. After all, I was leaving in the morning.

She tried a few cab companies but the lines just rang with no answer. Then her phone went dead again and she gave up. We started to talk again, the way we had out on that deck on the Monday I came into town.

"So what you gonna do?" I asked her.

"About what?"

"About your nigga? I mean, where you gonna live?"

She paused for a moment and returned her eyes to the front door she had entered nearly an hour before. She was looking for a way out. Her six-dollar-an-hour job couldn't take care of her, at least not the way she wanted. Her friends were few and far between. She had killed her man's baby and never told him and now she had run away from it all onto the couch where I had laid my head for a week. For her there was nothing to do but look for a way out. So she just sat there and stared at the door hoping that the answer would somehow magically come right through it. And surprisingly it did.

Boom! Boom! Each knock made the door rattle. I knew Robin couldn't knock that hard if she was using a metal pipe.

"Open the door, mothafucka!" the Terminator yelled from the other side of the doorframe.

While most people might have panicked, a smile glazed

dark

my lips. It was so unreal that I thought it was a joke. But I couldn't make myself actually laugh. I settled for the smile and the knowledge that whatever was about to happen was going to make it final.

Why the fuck won't this nigga leave me alone! I yelled to myself.

The door snapped off of its hinges and crashed onto the floor with a thud. It was a good thing that I hadn't paid a deposit.

I jumped to my feet but Alicia was way ahead of me as she tried to block him from entering.

"Nigga, what the fuck is wrong with you?" I yelled. "Kicking in doors and shit?"

He let out a growl where the words should have been and shoved Alicia to the side. She smacked against the wood floor like a spilled ice cube. He rushed at me and I sprung from the sofa and put my guard up, trying to think how I was going to get out of the apartment alive. I had taken a hit from him before and I didn't know if I could survive another one. He swung at my face but I backed out of the way, stumbling in the process and falling to the floor. Then he dove after me and missed again, giving me time to get back to my feet. I kicked him in the face and flattened him again. Blood dripped from his lower lip. I started looking for a weapon.

I didn't see anything anywhere that could put him down for the ten count except for the unplugged steam iron that was all the way over by the door. I ran towards it but I stubbed my toe on the end of the sofa and hit the floor cheek first. I looked up for the clock that told me how many seconds I had left before I got stomped.

But from the corner of my eye I saw the butt of the Beretta poking out from behind the ruffle beneath the sofa and I reached for it just as he got to me. I got a firm grip and pointed it at the Terminator. He froze. Then it was his turn to smile.

"Go ahead, little nigga! C'mon, your little bitch ass ain't gonna shoot me!"

He took me for some chump from the suburbs that didn't know the golden rule: If you pull a gun you better be ready to shoot it. And I was ready. I was also tired. I was tired of running and boxing with this big light-skinned bama who shouldn't have had a beef with me in the first place. I didn't even want his girl. I wanted the twenty-three-year-old girl with the round ass and the nice titties who lived down the hall.

"You better do somethin'! You better not miss! 'Cuz if you miss I'ma kill you!"

He needed to shut up. He didn't know that I had pulled the trigger before. I had placed that bullet right in the middle of Nick's skull and I could do it again. All he had to do was collect his girl and leave. My index finger tightened around the trigger. The safety was already off. I had to show him what he wasn't expecting to see.

But then in my mind I watched us drive away from Nick's corpse in that alley and I saw my faceless mama breathing her last breath on the way to a hospital she never

dark

lived to see. I thought about what Pop had said about all it took was one shot. My first shot had already done enough. Nick had only been guilty of taking the ass he had been offered. My finger loosened.

It really didn't have to do with the preacher's sermon or Nick or my mama or Pop or any of the things that were changing my life while it happened. It had to do with me. As I looked Diamelo the Terminator in the eye all I could see was what I had been. The dark figure in my dreams with the .380 now wore my face. Behind my target's eyes was that presence that had sent Snowflake, Cuckoo, me, and my father to the Dark Side. He had come through my door possessed by that dark demon that erased all ethics and reason and thirsted only for blood in exchange for a final closure.

I had been him. I too had come through a doorway to find betrayal. Sure, he was wrong about what he saw, but our reactions had been the same. He was only doing what he felt he had to and I didn't fault him for that.

But before I could lower the gun he took a smack at it. My arm uncontrollably swung to the left and my index finger squeezed twice. Two bullets pierced the far wall next to where the front door had been.

"Oh shit!" a voice yelled outside the door, and the fight paused. Bill crawled past the doorway on his back. The left of his white T-shirt was soaked with blood. All three of us watched in horror at the way his feet scrambled against the linoleum as he tried to get up.

I sprinted to the doorway as fast as I could to see that he had been hit in the shoulder. Blood ran down his arm and streaked across the floor. I didn't know what to do except try to stop the bleeding. When I reentered the apartment Diamelo had thawed and looked as if he wasn't finished. He stood as tall as ever in front of me as if the bleeding man in the hall no longer mattered. In one motion I stopped, reached and grabbed the iron from the doorway, and smashed him in the face with it. He fell backwards and landed with his eyes closed and blood flowing freely from his now-broken nose.

I ran to the bathroom and tore my bath towel in half to make a tourniquet and ran back to the hallway, where I made it as tight as I could around Bill's bloody arm. I had seen that in a movie on TV. But Bill had passed out.

His body still trembled, and I hoped that I wasn't hurting him more as I dragged him down the three flights of steps to the car. I wasn't going to let him die. I dragged him across the backseat and started the car.

"Happy anniversary, baby!" he murmured suddenly as I pulled off. I ran through the first and only stoplight.

The hospital was already in view before I thought about Alicia and Diamelo and the fact that there was blood in the hallway and that my door had been kicked in because of one man's insecurity. Would someone call the cops or would Alicia be smart enough to at least wipe up the blood so that I might not go to jail for something or other? The gun was still somewhere on the floor. Would one of them use it on the other? Would Robin walk in and see the whole thing? Would E show up and help me cover my tracks? Would I get to go to heaven after all of this? I'd have to deal with that in the next episode, because at present all the questions sang an annoying nursery rhyme in my mind that had begun to drive me crazy. But as long as Bill was breathing I was okay.

I remembered where the hospital was because I had ended up there the first time I was trying to find the library. The emergency room was near the first parking lot entrance on the right. I swerved into the lot and double-parked at the entrance. Two lunch-breaking paramedics dropped their sandwiches to get Bill on a stretcher while I, claiming to be his nephew, went through his wallet to get all the info I needed for the six forms I had to fill out. They carted him off to an operating room and left me to properly park the car and wait.

As I paced outside in front of the emergency room entrance I tried to piece together what had happened. Bill must have heard the door get kicked in and come to investigate. One of the bullets that went through the wall had lodged in his shoulder as he was walking by. He had fallen down in shock from the wound.

A white cop with a red neck materialized before me two hours later. He was short, five-eight at best, and had that doughnut-inspired paunch that all cops get. There was no partner, which struck me as strange.

"I understand you brought in a gunshot victim," he said as he produced a pen and pad.

"Yeah," I replied. "I came into my building and I saw my super on the stairs. And he was bleeding. So I dragged him down to my car and brought him here."

"Did you hear any gunshots? Any noise?"

"No, but I did have my system up real loud, so I might've missed it. Have you talked to him yet?"

"No, he's still in surgery. I have to get your name."

"Charles Smith. I live at 2220 Tryon, Apartment 2C. If you need anything else, officer, feel free to come by. I don't have a phone. Couldn't pay the bill, you know?"

I gave an innocent smile that might have won me an Oscar. He looked me over thoroughly before he swallowed the story whole. I knew they wouldn't come by the building. Bill was alive and wasn't pressing charges. Doughnuts were a more important thing to do. It'd take them at least a day to make a house call and by then I'd be gone.

"We'll be in touch if we need you," he replied. I extended my hand and shook his and he walked through the automatic doors that led to the parking lot. I exhaled, dumbfounded by how easy it was to fool a cop. Or maybe he had just been testing me. Maybe he was waiting out in the lot with six other cops in three other cars. That would have been fitting, to come hundreds of miles to avoid one crime only to get caught up in another, to be enslaved in the promised land.

But now that Charlotte's finest were out of the way, the tricky part was to figure out what had happened after I dragged Bill out the front door. I called E and he told me that he was already on his way to the building for damage control. I told him that I would wait for Bill's status and then go back to help him tie up any and all cover-up activities. As long as dark there were no cops or dead bodies there we were both pretty sure we could smooth it over.

Ray's Beretta had been broken in on an innocent by-stander who I might have called my friend. Maybe the infamous Toni would send him some flowers or even come by the hospital.

I'd gotten too used to guns in the recent months. At home the shots permeated the night as casually as a dog's barking. But now I'd done some capping. And in doing so I'd managed to bring myself closer to the only friend of mine I was sure I'd never be like.

It was our tenth-grade year and we had heard the shots from the other side of the playground. Everyone else on the court scattered like dropped marbles, but E and I stood frozen on the blacktop next to the bouncing unclaimed b-ball. The night before, Snow had told us that he was going to do it.

Shaka and his boys had come down to the playground, our playground, and shot at him. Snow was to be an example that someone else was taking over the neighborhood crack game. He was barely eighteen at the time and he just ran the product from place to place for enough money to get by. His mama was workin' two jobs and his dad and his brother were both locked up. Shaka's bullets were meant to shred all his dreams.

They had missed. Snow wouldn't. He came back to the court the next day with his brother's .38 and an attitude. Snow didn't tell the dudes he was running for about what had happened. He just reacted.

They were on the other side of the playground behind the jungle gym and the rec center. They stood in the same spot Snow had been designated to hold down until he was shot at the day before. There were four of them and none of them got to move another inch from where they were standing. The shots went off consecutively and when we saw him emerge from behind the playground equipment we knew he hadn't been playing. On the back staircase of E's building he had promised that they would die before the streetlights came on.

"Y'all wanna see the bodies?" he asked less than a hundred yards from the scene of the crime. Not a nerve on him twitched and his lips almost formed a grin. There was something in his eyes that scared me, a presence that hadn't been with him before that chilled me.

"Nah man, you better get outta here," E said in a voice that said he was as scared as I was. "We ain't seen nothin'."

"I know you didn't," he replied coldly as he turned and walked toward the playground entrance and then across the street toward his building.

"We better roll too," E said to me.

"Yeah," I replied from my fifteen-year-old lips. But my legs didn't move and my eyes continued to study the afterimage of that something in Snow's eyes. Minutes later when E had given up on me and headed back to his building I crossed the playground and saw all four of the corpses. Their bodies still twitched as the last atoms of life vacated the scene. Bill had twitched that way when I dragged him down the steps. Dried blood stained my hands. I took a seat and closed my eyes.

I was leaving with a sore jaw and a stubbed toe, having

dark

shot the building super and clobbered an unreasonably jealous boyfriend with an iron. A girl who was a self-proclaimed killer kept getting me in trouble with a dude I didn't have any real problems with. I was sure I would probably go to hell for killing Nick and Robin had disappeared and someone might have died in a domestic dispute at my apartment while I was trying to take an innocent bystander to the hospital. My mama was dead. My main boy had a brand-new life and my car needed a new muffler. My vacation in Charlotte hadn't exactly been what I'd expected.

In retrospect I almost couldn't believe that the DC police hadn't even come close to implicating me or anyone in my crew for Nick's murder. I also couldn't believe I had gotten with the finest girl I had ever been with and been offered a chance to change my life for the better. Charlotte had given me a little bit of everything and I wanted to tell Pop about it all, write it down and let him read it later the way Robin was doing with her mama. So I got a pen and pad from the nurse at the desk and wrote something I wouldn't give to Pop for a long time.

"bam! bam! i smoked you!"

a little boy said to me, pointing his water gun in my direction. I had been waiting for ninety minutes and the boy's mother had been waiting just as long. She stood outside at the curb of the emergency room entrance looking for a car that didn't seem like it would show up. I looked down at the little kid and his gun and shook my head. That was where it had all started.

We got our little water pistols and dart guns so we could pretend we were the A Team or the guy from *Lethal Weapon* or *Hunter* or whoever. It had all been a game. It still was.

When I didn't say anything the little boy ran down to the end of the sidewalk and squirted at an imaginary enemy. Then the car they had been waiting for creeped into the parking lot and the two of them departed.

"he's going to be okay," someone in a white coat and stethoscope told me inside twenty minutes later. The bullet had actually lodged in his collarbone but they had gotten it out. They were keeping him for a day or two, mainly because of the shock. He was still asleep, but since I was *family* I was told that I could see him.

I followed the doctor through two sets of swinging doors to an elevator and then to a room where Bill was sleeping in a baby surgical gown. He had hair on his shoulders. The bandage for the wound was thick and fluffy.

"I'm sorry, man," I said.

"How did this happen?" the doctor asked me.

"I don't know. I came home and he was laying in the hallway shot. Wasn't nobody else around."

"The police—"

dark

"They asked me some questions outside. I just live in his building. They said they'd be back later."

"I understand," the doctor said, "but I have to ask."

"It's okay," I said. "But I'ma let him sleep. I'll be back in a few hours."

"Okay," the doctor said, faking a smile as he walked out before me.

Bill didn't move an inch during the fifteen minutes I stood there listening to the beeps on the EKG machine. The thick stubble on his face was two days away from being a beard and you could tell by the lines in his face that he had seen more than I wanted to think about. I was young but when we talked there had been that something between us. I wanted more than anything to say that he was my friend, but I didn't know him well enough. He was just the super who had jumped in the way of my stray bullet.

"I'll be back, man," I said as I walked out.

Between Bill's room and the car I saw another gunshot victim, an eight-year-old kid vomiting uncontrollably, and a teenage white girl who looked like she had a broken arm. Everyone on the planet has some kind of a problem.

I drove back to the building with the radio off and the windows down. As I whisked back down Tryon I could hear the crickets singing at ten to eleven on a Sunday night. A cigarette and some sleep would make me feel better. But I had a feeling I might not get either.

"he didn't die or anything, did he?"

E asked as he sprayed 409 on the last of the bloodstains on the staircase and wiped it up with a browning rag.

"Nah, bullet broke his collarbone. They supposed to let him out tomorrow or Tuesday. I'ma go see him again in the mornin'. Were they still up there when you got here?"

"Nah, just left the door layin' there in the living room. The gun was in the corner but wasn't nobody there. Ma's gonna be pissed about the door."

I dug into my pocket and counted off a hundred dollars from my bankroll but E waved it away.

"Don't worry 'bout it. Ma always keeps one or two extra doors in the basement. I just wonder if Bill can fix it with a bullet hole in him."

"He can fix anything he wants to," I said.

"What you 'bout to do?" he asked.

"Go up and get some sleep," I said.

"You ain't got no door."

"I got fifteen shots though. That's better than a door."

"So you still leavin' tomorrow?"

"Got to."

"Did Ma talk to you?"

"Yeah. I got a lot of things to think about."

"I know," he said. "Just holler at me when you get home."

"You know it," I said. We hugged the way brothers do   dark
and went in opposite directions on the staircase. We didn't

need to say anything else. We never ever said goodbye. At least that hadn't changed.

The apartment was surprisingly neat for a place where a brawl and shooting had taken place. Everything was where I had left it. E had stashed the Beretta back under the sofa and I let it stay there.

I walked over to the nightstand and wrote a note for Robin. It read:

I'm leaving tomorrow and I want to say goodbye before I go.

—Thai

I folded it and put it between the door and the doorframe of Apartment 3F and then went back to 3C and closed my eyes on the couch. I faded to black in no time.

My last dream in Charlotte was another nightmare. I was running through the apartment building trying to get away from Bill, Sierra, Nick, and my mother, who ran towards me backwards so I couldn't see her face. They followed me through every door and window and turned up around every corner until they had me trapped in the laundry room. That was when a tongue and a pair of teeth woke me up.

The tongue tickled my lips and then pressed its way into my mouth. Then her lips covered mine and my eyes popped open. My dick rose like a flagpole. She gave me that porn star look with her eyes that made me want her more than I already had. Still without a word she straddled me and took her tongue back long enough to speak.

"You know I missed you," she said. "Must be losing my touch."

"I missed you too," I replied. She backed away.

"I wasn't expectin' to hear that."

"Neither was I, but tomorrow I'll be gone and I want you to know that I wish things was different, that I had some more time."

"Why you gotta leave?" she asked. "It's just startin' to get fun. We're both startin' to have somethin' to lose. You know that every time I leave I wonder if you'll be here when I get back, and now I know that the next time you won't."

"I wish I didn't have to go. But I got some things to take care of at home," I said.

"You ever comin' back?" she asked with a concern I hadn't heard before.

I paused before I answered. "That's what I wanted to ask you about." I put my hands on her hips and pulled her close to me and held on.

"What you wanna ask me about?"

"If you had a chance to just move and go somewhere and start over and do what you wanted to do almost for free, would you?"

"It depends," she said as she ran her fingers across my stubbly face, "on what I would have to give up. Why?"

dark

"I got this chance to move down here and get in school

and get a job and just start over, but I don't wanna leave all my peoples in the neighborhood behind."

She laughed like Pop did when I said something stupid. "You ain't leavin' nobody," she said. "Your whole neighborhood can come with you if they want. You ain't stoppin' them from doin' that. But I think you know that you gotta do your own thing. You gotta make your dreams happen and go after what you want, 'cuz they won't stop for you. I know I ain't stoppin' for nobody. It sounds to me like you ain't doin' nothin' at home anyway."

"I ain't," I said, "and I got this bad feelin' that the longer I stay there the more problems I'ma have."

"Then you answered your own question," she said. "But look, if this is our last night forever then let's go down the hall and say goodbye."

"But wait."

"What?"

"Even if I don't come back, can I call you?"

She nodded and scribbled her number down on the newspaper on the coffee table.

She took my hand and led me to 3F, where for three hours she showed me things I hadn't learned in Rounds 1 and 2.

leaving

rays of sunlight
shot through Robin's bedroom window. I popped up like toast and got dressed while she was still asleep. On my way out I stared at her sleeping face for what seemed like a long time and then went back over and kissed her on the cheek.

We had said what we each needed to. There didn't have to be a final kiss and she wouldn't have to chase me to my car to stop me from leaving. I wrote my number and address on a Post-it and left it on her computer screen on my way out.

I rumbled down the stairs like a locomotive trying to

figure out what I had to do first. Part of me was already speeding up I-85 while the other part was ready to start the day like it had been any other. In that short trip down the staircase I had blocked out the night before. I had blocked out Bill, Alicia, and especially Diamelo. But when I landed in the lobby it all came back again as he stood right in front of me.

From ten feet away I thought that the Terminator was back for the sequel. His eyes were bloodshot and his nose was taped and bandaged. The right hand that poked out of his wrinkled dress shirt was wrapped in gauze. He looked as if he'd been standing in the same spot for hours.

"She's gone," he said solemnly in a voice I hadn't expected him to use. "Said she ain't never want to see me again. She ran out and I couldn't catch her."

"Why you here? Why you tellin' me for?" I asked.

" 'Cuz you here," he said. "You know you broke my nose in two places. But I ain't tryin' to fight no more."

"What happened to your hand? I know I ain't do that."

"Car was out of gas so I just started walkin' after she ran off. I was so mad I started punchin' stop signs on the street. Cracked three knuckles. You in love with her?"

"Love who?"

"You love Alicia?"

"I don't even know Alicia. I met her like a few days ago. We ain't really even friends."

"You wasn't tryin' to fuck her?"

"Nah, man."

dark

230

"But I seen her take you out to the river. That's where me and her used to go when we first got together."

"I can't speak on that. We just talked."

"You know I just seen y'all down there and I kept thinkin' you was gonna fuck her and I followed you back to your buildin'."

"How'd you know where I stayed?"

"I followed you the first day you was talkin' to her at the mall and from there I followed you and your boy to your buildin'. Then I looked up and I saw you in the third-floor window and figured out that was where you lived. So I went up there and when you came in I hit you in the face to get you to stay away from my baby."

"You know if this was where I'm from you'd be dead now. But to be honest I don't care about you or her. I just wanna get my life straight."

"You ever been in love?" he asked, taking a few steps towards me.

"Nah," I replied. "Don't wanna be either."

"You shouldn't. I'm twenty-four years old and this is my first time. If nobody ever told you, it's the greatest thing in the world but it makes you do crazy things. 'Cuz I love her I'll do anything for her. You know I might even kill for her."

"Man, you ain't gotta tell me all this."

"I'm just tellin' you 'cuz you here. I'm supposed to be at work but I been walkin' around all night. Is that old man that got shot all right?"

"I think so. I'm 'bout to go see right now."

"That's good."

As he stood in front of me he didn't look like the kind of man to be growling or kicking in doors. His demon had been exorcised.

"I didn't mean to kick your door in or none of that stuff at the club. But when I get a little liquor in me it's like I'm a different person. When it's about her I just lose it."

"I know what you mean," I said. "I know what you mean."

We talked for another twenty minutes, about nothing. With my gas can I gave him enough fuel to get his cherry-red '98 Acura started up. In the interim I learned that he had just graduated from Johnson C. Smith in May and he had an internship at a bank downtown. He wanted to get into banking and he had first seen Alicia when she came in to open an account at the branch where he was working as a teller. I could have seen bouncing, but banking? Then again I'd also seen an Indian woman catch the Holy Ghost and my super talk to doors. But with his injuries he'd definitely be working in the vault for a while.

On the magical day that they met he followed her across the street to the mall and gave it his best shot, and for the first time in his life it had worked. His parents were well off, so aside from his relatively small salary he could still afford to give her everything she wanted. She had reeled him in slowly and after a while the word "no" was removed from his vocabulary.

Sierra had had me under that same spell, and when her spell broke on that living room floor I didn't have anything left but that same fire I had seen in his eyes. He saw that in me too. As we talked he seemed smaller. It was best he didn't know about the baby.

We had a quick laugh towards the end about how fast I could run.

"Damn, my eyes is red," he said as he studied them in his rearview. Apparently he had neglected to look at everything else. "I have to go to CVS and get some Visine so I don't go to work looking like a vampire."

I kept my comments to myself. We both drove off towards downtown. I was pretty sure that I would never see him again.

Traffic on the way to the hospital was heavy. It was slightly after nine on a Monday morning and once again all the world's weekend passes had expired. I didn't feel like paying for parking so I stashed the car a few blocks up in a shopping center and walked down.

I slithered through the swinging doors and up the stairs and finally into the elevator that took me to Bill's room. He was wide awake this time, trying to eat what looked like eggs off a hospital plate. But he dropped his fork when he saw me.

"Don't tell me you was the one that shot me," he asked, grinning.

"Yeah and no. See, I shot the wall. The bullet shot you. You was just in the wrong place."

"Yeah, I bet. So you ain't even gonna apologize?"

"I been sayin' I'm sorry since I brought you in here last night. You all right?"

"You shot me, youngblood, but besides this big-ass bandage on my shoulder I guess I'm okay."

"Well, I'm 'bout to go back home. I just wanted to check on you."

"Shoot and run, huh? Let me stop messin' wit' you. I'm sorry to see you go. You one of the first people in that buildin' I liked talkin' to. But let me ask you somethin'."

"What?"

"You find what you lookin' for while you was here?"

"What you mean?"

"I ain't one of the Three Wise Men. Think about it and see what you come up with. I know you smart. You just used to people always givin' you the answers," he said.

"Who's Toni?" I asked, avoiding the effort it would have taken to give him an answer.

"I told you I don't want to talk about that."

"Hey, I brought you to the hospital."

"But you was the one that shot me." We both laughed again.

"Nah, for real. Is she your girl or somethin'?"

"Little more than that, youngblood. More than that. She's my wife. She used to live wit' me in the buildin'. She left me about three months ago. Said I drink too much."

"How long was y'all married?"

"Two years. See, she was a young girl. Thirty-four or thirty-five. Married me when I was still runnin' my company. I was makin' a nice piece of change then too. I think she thought I was richer than I was, but I'll give it to her, when I got hit with that lawsuit and lost it all she hung in there with me for richer or poorer. But then I started drinkin'. I mean I went all out for a long time and we fought

234

about it all the time. Then it got to the point where when I got drunk she locked me out the apartment till I was sober. Then one day, May fifteenth, 1997, to be exact, she locked me out and then went out down the fire escape and never came back. Least she left a note. Told me I could find her when I was ready to deal with things. Left an address where I could write her, but I ain't never wrote."

"Why not?"

"I ain't ready to deal with things. I'm fifty-five years old. More than half my life is over but I still got all this stuff hangin'. Some of it is things I did when I didn't know no better. Others is just plain outright stupidity. When it gets bad they eat away at me while I sleep at night and I always wake up missin' a part of me. Without Toni I'll never be whole again. That's why I keep lookin' for her.

"Some nights I'll hear her cryin' in that apartment next to the one I'm in now. See, me and her used to live in 3D and when I'm drunk I can hear her yellin' real loud. So I go over there and I knock, hopin' that she'll hear me. But she never does. Next thing I remember I'm back in my bed lookin' for something to get me through the night, especially when I ain't got no repairs to do. Hell, when you shot me I was on my way to get me a nice fifth. Now you got me sober and I'm more worried about this damn bullet wound than anything else. Guess I really wasn't no alcoholic after all."

"When they lettin' you out?" I asked.

"Said I can leave this afternoon," he replied as he leaned back in his bed. "Shit, I ain't got hurt in so long I'm glad them insurance people gon' actually get to spend some

dark

235

money on me. I almost wanna say thank you for shootin' me. Got me a two-week vacation. Ol' Ms. Mehdi had her son call a little while ago to let me know."

"Don't mention it. I'll shoot you again the next time I get a chance," I said. "You know I'm leavin' today."

"You said that already. You want me to throw you a party or somethin'? You ever comin' back?"

"I might be around," I said.

"I'll take that as a yes. Think you like it here a little bit."

"You might be right. But I ain't tellin' you one way or another."

"If I was you I wouldn't tell me neither," he said. "But if you leavin' you need to get your narrow ass outta here. Don't worry about me. You take care of you and you'll be all right. You got a good brain, you just gotta learn how to use it, been spendin' too much time lettin' other people think for you."

"I will," I said, turning toward the exit.

"And one more thing," he said with his good arm raised. "Quit smokin' them damn cigarettes all the time. You too young to be getting your lungs all black."

"All right. But you better quit too. You too old to have your lungs black too."

"Difference is I ain't gotta use 'em as long as you do. But I'll keep that in mind," he said. I nodded and disappeared through the exit.

The Charlotte heat had risen early on my last day in town. I thought I saw my spit sizzle as I hocked it onto the ten-o'clock concrete. I thought to call Ms. Mehdi but she'd told me to take as much time as I needed so I didn't rush. But

I did call my job to say that my flight got canceled. No one was having a heart attack about my absence.

The door to Apartment 3C was reattached when I returned, but the locks didn't work and one hinge held it more strongly than the other. I suspected that it was E's carpentry. It would hold until Bill could do a better job.

I stuffed everything into my gym bag and slid the Beretta and clip in separate side pockets. I unplugged my alarm clock, wound up the cord, and sat it on top of the bag along with my radio. Then I stacked all the week's newspapers I had bought into a small pile and carried them downstairs to the recycling bin. When I came back up I was exhausted. I layed down on the sofa to rest my eyes. Sharp rays of sunlight beamed in from both windows. I was so tired that I didn't even dream.

"thai,"

a high-pitched happy-sounding voice whispered, "Thai, are you all right?"

I was so groggy and confused that I thought it was my mother. But as I opened my eyes into the still-piercing sunlight overhead I saw that the voice belonged to Qualie Madison.

She stood over me grinning like a child on Christmas morning. I hadn't seen her since the day we had dinner, and I had almost forgotten that she existed.

"Are you all right?" she asked again in that voice that was whiter than white itself. I nodded affirmatively.

"What happened last night?" she said.

"What do you mean? Who told you something happened?" I couldn't believe it. I was almost out and she was pulling me back in.

"Nobody told me anything, but I saw you putting Bill in your car last night when I was coming home from work. There was blood everywhere."

"I don't know. I just found him on the stairwell and he was bleeding so I took him to the hospital. Turned out somebody shot him. But I didn't know that you and Bill were tight."

I got to my feet and went to the refrigerator, forgetting that it was empty. I was more parched than before.

"Bill just comes up to use my iron sometimes," she said. "But is he all right?"

"Yeah, I went to see him this morning. He was kinda out of it but I wanted to tell him goodbye."

"You're leaving?"

"Yeah, around two or three," I replied.

"You sure didn't stay here too long."

"My week is up. This was just a vacation. Now I gotta go back to work."

"I don't even know where you work. I don't know anything about you."

"It's probably better that way, Qualie," I said. "But who knows? You might see me again."

She was in her bartender uniform: black pants and vest and a white shirt. Her now-platinum blond hair was pinned up and her eyes were drenched in mascara.

"So did you get a better job?" I asked.

"No, I decided to stay where the money was," she replied as she sat down on the other end of the couch and scratched her nose with her index finger. "Even if most of it was coming from g-strings and perverts."

"You gotta do what you gotta do," I said.

"I guess, but I just wish things didn't have to be the way they are. Why does it all have to be so complicated?"

"I couldn't tell you," I said. "You just never know what you're gonna be doin'."

"You never did tell me why you came here," she said.

"I just came to see some friends, nothin' complicated."

"Well I'm sorry we didn't get to hang out more."

I wasn't. "Well, thanks for the dinner anyway."

"You're more than welcome. I'd like to make it for you again sometime."

We talked for a few more minutes but no matter how hard I tried her words floated away like helium balloons. But it wasn't her fault. In twenty minutes we were both once again staring off in opposite directions of the apartment.

Too many dudes I knew would have tried to fuck Qualie the first night she invited them to dinner. But from what little I knew I already had a good idea of what her story was, and it didn't interest me in the least. Besides, I had Robin. I didn't need anyone else.

Qualie left me in my apartment the same way she'd found me sixty minutes earlier. I barely stayed awake long enough to hear the conclusion to her goodbye address. She told me to give her a ring if I ever blew into Charlotte again. I told her I would even though I only feigned writing her number down.

When my eyelids opened again it was way past three. I was late. I grabbed my bag, my alarm clock, and my radio and rushed down the stairs to get to the car. But someone was waiting for me in the lobby.

Alicia had changed into a red dress. Her eyes matched the color of the fabric. She leaned against the lobby doorframe like someone who was out of breath.

"I had just about given up on you."

"I ain't know I was supposed to be here," I said.

"I wanted to see you before you left and to say I'm sorry."

"For what? 'Cuz you lied? 'Cuz your boy kicked in my fuckin' door? 'Cuz he made me shoot somebody? 'Cuz I been fighting and running all over the city 'cuz your nigga got the wrong idea? That why you sorry?"

"Yeah," she said. "I dumped him this morning."

"He told me. He don't look like he's taking it too well."

"I didn't come with a guarantee. He knew that."

I shook my head. "You know it seem like you care more about how I feel than how he does, and he was your man."

"You don't understand!"

"You right. I don't. I don't even want to understand. All I'm tryin' to do is get home."

"So you really leavin'?"

"I got bags in my hand, don't I?"

"Look, I really need you to be my friend."

"What the hell for? You don't know what bein' friends is about. I got friends who'll take a bullet for me. I got friends who'll give me a place to stay and make sure I don't never go hungry. Is you one of them kind of friends? I don't think you are, and to be honest I really don't need you. I got enough to deal wit' when I get back anyway."

"I didn't mean to—"

"You didn't mean to what? I mean you got a older dude with a good-ass job running around chasin' me and kickin' in my door 'cuz he love you so much and you need a friend? Sound like you got a better friend than me already. But look, I gotta roll. . . ."

"I don't know where I'm staying tomorrow!" she exploded. "My cousins is out of town. I got five dollars in my pocket and I gotta be to work in ninety minutes."

"That's a pretty big problem. But it's your problem. The door to 3C is open but that's all I can tell you. I ain't one of your free rides. Super comes back tomorrow. I hope God's looking out for you." I started walking past her.

"Thank you," she said humbly. My back was to her as I headed for the front doorway. She had done her baby a favor.

"You ever comin' back?" she asked.

"Yeah," I said, "I'll be back."

I turned and went through the lobby doors and out into the hot Charlotte street. I wished I hadn't shown up at Sierra's fifteen minutes early. I wished I hadn't pulled that trigger. I wished my mama had lived long enough to teach me more about girls, and I wished that Ms. Mehdi's offer hadn't been too good to refuse. The sunlight beamed down on me like the Word of God and I hoped that there was some way I'd get to heaven when it was all said and done.

I loaded the trunk of my Maxima with the missing hub-cap and then I lit my last Newport ever and dropped the rest of the pack on the ground. As I started the car I thought about what I had learned from Ms. Diane Brown, my seventh-grade science teacher. She said that change was a constant and that every action had an equal and opposite re-action. I had run from murdering Nick Washington and now I was going back home.

I had to go back. I had promises to keep, to Pop, to Snow, and to myself. If I could return home, to the belly of the beast, where there was an unsolved murder, potential retri-bution, and other mysteries abounding, and remain un-scathed, then would I be worthy to walk out of Shaw's wilderness onto the cleared path that led to my own Manifest Destiny. Only then could Thai Williams, with his murder, and his scars, and his love, return to the place called Char-lotte, the next in a list of many places that he would call home.